COZY CHRISTMAS CRIMES

WENDY H. JONES   SHEENA MACLEOD   MARTI M. MCNAIR

Scott and Lawson Publishing

CONTENTS

INTRODUCTION

I am a sucker for Christmas especially a Christmas book or a Christmas movie. It somehow makes me feel all nostalgic and many other readers feel the same way. Cozy Christmas Crime books have it all - nostalgia, mystery, great characters and a feeling of being on the safe side of murder. What more could we want. Cozy is challenging to write as the main character cannot have any help from the police or any other law enforcement. Rather than forensics, it is nosiness, snooping and gut instinct that are employed. Whilst it does make it difficult for the writer, they are both fun to write and fun for the reader.

I love to read a cozy mystery, and when that is twinned with food and recipes to die for - quite literally in the cases in this book - then seventh heaven comes to mind. Do not worry, the recipes are all poison free and the most dangerous thing that might happen is you will die laughing or maybe pull a muscle. Happy reading.

CHRISTMAS BOOKS CAN BE MURDER

Wendy H. Jones

When bookshop owner Holly MacLaren hosts a festive wine and mystery night with her best friend Anastasia, the last thing she expects is a real-life murder. But when scathing newspaper critic Timothy Bombast drops dead among the mince pies, and a priceless rare book vanishes, Holly and Anastasia must channel their inner Miss Marples to solve the case. With a town full of secrets, a missing first edition of *The Mysterious Affair at Styles*, and Holly's police officer boyfriend caught between duty and love, can the amateur sleuths crack the case before Christmas is cancelled and their reputations, and that of the newly formed bookshop, are ruined?

Death had not been invited to the party but strolled in anyway, brushing snow off his hood and looking for more than a mince pie and a glass of cheap prosecco.

Not that Holly MacLaren realised this yet, so she planned the party in blissful ignorance. Bookshops are not the place one usually associates with murder, unless on the mystery shelves, meaning her sense of confidence was entirely appropriate. She was employed in decorating the shop for not only Christmas, but one of the most highly anticipated book launches of the year. Holly, the owner of Firtown's most prestigious bookshop, Cozy Up with a Book, had landed the coup of the century – Melissa Nestor, the world's most well-loved Christmas book writer, had agreed to launch *Snow-Tinged Love* at the shop.

The door opened to the sound of 'Oh Christmas Tree'. Holly, dressed as an elf, leapt out from her spot behind the real Christmas Tree. 'Ho, Ho. Ho, how can...' Before she could finish, she was swept into a bear hug by an enormous man with a bushy beard; no, not Santa but the town's hottest police officer, and Holly's boyfriend, Danny Cooper. Although he was known to do a stint or two as Father Christmas at the town's various events.

A smaller figure clutched at her legs. 'Daddy says I can come to your party tonight.' Blonde ponytails swung hither and thither as she leapt around emitting squeaks that would make the most vocal of mice jealous.

Danny said, 'Actually, little Miss Morag, I said you could come for half an hour and then your babysitter would be taking you home to bed.' He laughed at the sight of his daughter's pout and tweaked her nose. 'Five-year-old girls need lots of sleep if they are to grow even more cute.'

'I'm cute. I'm cute.' Morag dashed around the shop, breaking into a spirited rendition of Jingle Bells. Hemingway, the book-shop's enormous ginger cat, followed at her heels. He'd grown from a tiny scrap of fur and bones who had to be fed via a dropper, to an animal who would not be out of place in the local zoo. Holly had tried to take him home numerous times, but the bibliophile feline would rather be knocking books off shelves than knocking back fillet steak in her pad.

Holly caught the bright-eyed elf in a hug as the door once more chimed out its seasonal ring tone. A woman, as wide as she was tall, staggered in holding a box which, by the look on her face, weighed more than any sane person should be carrying. She placed the box on the antique table in the middle of the room, dislodging a copy of Agatha Christie's *The Mysterious Affair at Styles* in the process.

'That's a first edition,' Holly dashed over to the table and snatched the priceless book out of harm's way.'

'Sorry.' Anastasia Lang, award winning sommelier and Holly's best friend, could not look less sorry if she tried. 'Mixed case of local wines. There's another box in the car and a mixed box of Californian and Australian. Danny, could you flex those muscles of yours and bring the other two boxes in?'

Danny trotted off to oblige. Anastasia looked around the room her eyes wide. You've worked wonders in here. How you've managed to blend Victorian and contemporary themes, making them both work, should be one of the wonders of the world.' She sniffed the air. 'Is that mince pies I can smell?'

'Got it in one. No party would be complete without Mama MacLaren's famous mince pies.'

'Is Mama herself coming to the soiree?'

'Are you kidding? Melissa Nestor is her favourite author; she'll be the first one through the door.'

Said door opened once more, and Danny rushed through it bearing two boxes of wine with ease. He deposited them on the correct table and moved their sibling to join them. He then collected his daughter, kissed Holly on the cheek and said he would see her later. His eyes simultaneously twinkled and indicated he loved her – no mean feat to achieve.

Holly tackled the remainder of the decorating whilst Anastasia did what she did best – titivated the table with bottles, wine glasses, champagne flutes, and ice buckets. The finished result could have graced a table at Buckingham Palace. Taking a last look around and approving of every bit of it, Holly locked the door and sped towards her house for a quick turnaround in the costume department. Elves certainly wouldn't be welcome at that night's get together. Not even a petite one sporting a perky, blonde ponytail.

Light from the chandeliers and strategically placed lanterns bounced off the assorted and exquisite jewels adorning the necks, ears and fingers of the elegantly dressed women. Ball-gowns in every hue and style competed with the tuxedos of the well-tailored men. Firtown had pulled out all the stops to match the elegant theme of *Snow-Tinged Love*. Of course, Nestor herself was the most beautifully dressed of them all with a figure and hairstyle which would have the highest paid supermodels lurid green with envy. Despite her star status in the literary world, she mingled with the guests, greeting each fan like they were the most important person in the world. Her publisher, Stephen Tiernan, was glued to her side. Melissa turned and whispered something to him, and he took a couple of steps back, his face turning red. He pulled on his moustache and hopped from foot to foot.

'She knows how to work a room,' Holly whispered to Anastasia. 'But he's as useless as a proof copy in a bookshop. She grabbed a glass of merlot from the table, more as a prop than to drink. Holly could get drunk on the sniff of a barmaid's apron, and she needed every faculty she possessed on high alert to pull tonight off.

She shimmied over to Melissa. Before she could say one word her mother appeared, as if by magic, the light of fandom shining from her eyes. Holly was about to introduce her mother to the star when Timothy Bombast shoved them both aside and planted himself squarely in front of Nestor.

Holly, knowing this was about par for the course where the local journalist was concerned, resigned herself to waiting. She didn't have to wait long because Melissa, in the most charming of ways, managed to make him feel he was of the utmost importance whilst simultaneously handing him over to her assistant who twittered nearby. It was a definite skill; one Holly wished she had. Bombast's scathing reviews on everything from restaurants to books brought many a business to the brink of insolvency. His review of the local hairdressing salon Cut, Curl and Style, ended with one of the hairdressers having three weeks off with stress. Holly lived her life in fear of upsetting him. The assistant swiftly moved him aside. 'Let me get you some refreshments?'

'Call these refreshments. They are too awful to be called second rate and would struggle with third and fourth.'

Holly, whose 'multi-award-winning chef' mother had provided the buffet, bristled on her behalf. She hoped she hadn't heard. Shoving ill feeling for Bombast aside, she said, 'May I introduce you to my mother, Noelle MacLaren?' After hovering for a few seconds, she wandered off, leaving them in deep conversation about writing Christmas romance books. Holly was more of a murder mystery girl, but she'd read *Snow-Tinged Love* to prepare for the night's event. It wasn't half bad and had her thinking she might try some of the author's other books. *Hawaiian Christmas Love* sounded like a bit of escapism. She had fifty-two other titles to choose from, their celebrity being a prolific writer. Although Holly wondered how she managed to write so many Christmas books and keep them original. Perhaps that's why she sold books rather than writing them.

Nestor was a popular author, so the non-stop jingling of the bell above the door added a merry cadence to the proceedings as most of the village poured through the doors. Add to the mix, wine enthusiasts from both near and far, and the bookshop was fit to burst at its highly sophisticated seams.

'Do you think the wine will hold out?' Holly asked.

'As I have more stashed under the table, I jolly well hope so.' Anastasia handed over a couple of glasses of Prosecco to some thirsty readers and waved them towards a table groaning with mince pies and other festive goodies. 'Anyway, I've got several more boxes squirrelled in the boot of my car.' She smiled and handed a champagne glass of apple juice to an excited Morag who was leaping from foot to foot in front of the table.

Holly blew her friend an air kiss, grabbed Morag's hand, and elbowed her way through the crowds towards Danny.

'I love grown-up parties.' The happy child continued to chatter as Holly listened with one ear and used the other to keep track of what was happening in the room.

'Daddy, I've got cham… champ… fizzy juice.'

Danny smiled, the type only an adoring father could muster and said, 'I can see that. You're not my baby anymore.'

'I's a big girl.'

Before he could answer, the squealing of a mike had customers covering their ears and slopping drinks. Holly looked around, her eyebrows drawn in puzzlement. Only she should be using the mike, and they were several mince pies and a prosecco short of starting the interview. Her eyes widened as she took in the sight of Timothy Bombast, all flashy waistcoat and pinstripe trousers, clutching the mike in his sweaty hand. *What in the name of Father Christmas is he up to?* She clutched her stomach at the wave of queasiness that came over her. She simultaneously clutched Danny's arm.

He put a protective arm around her waist. 'What's up, Bookworm?' The use of his private name for her showed the depth of his concern.

Knowing the local bobbie was right there beside her had her standing up straight and proper blazing in no time. She took one determined step towards Bombast but was cut off in mid-stride by the man himself.

'I was invited to give a review of *Snow-Tinged Love* by Festive Publications—'

'I can assure you, we did not—' Simon Garret, Nestor's esteemed publisher, looked at his mince pie like it was going to leap up and bite him. He took a swig of champagne, coughed and sprayed it everywhere, leaving his neighbours utilising napkins to dab at their clothes. All this did was transfer mince pie crumbs to their clothing – not the vibe Holly was going for.

Bombast, ignoring the publisher's protestations, continued, 'On being invited to this party, I made the decision to give my review of this woeful novel here.' He looked around the room as though considering a particularly nasty specimen of rotten fish. 'Although I cannot understand why I accepted. I'm used to a much higher calibre of venue.'

'He didn't get an invitation,' Holly whispered, too scared of the critic to speak the words any louder.

Gasps and horrified murmurs swept the room, swelling to a crescendo. Bombast screamed into the mike, 'Silence. I'm speaking, and you despicable specimens of humanity will listen.'

Cue collective jaw-dropping and instant hush, more at his arrogance than obedience.

'This book is possibly the worst I have had the misfortune to read and is fit for nothing other than an incinerator. The word puerile sprang to mind the instant I started, and I quickly knew it was the worst of Melissa Nestor's worthless collection of bilge.'

Holly scrubbed at her eyes in a vain attempt to stop tears flowing. Morag, having no clue what was going on, grabbed Holly's hand. Neither she nor Holly knew whether it was to comfort or be comforted. Danny, now in full policeman mode, started towards the critic before stopping dead in his tracks when Bombast grabbed his chest and dropped to the floor.

Miriam Vagus, the local GP, rushed to the stricken man, knelt down and felt for a pulse. 'Phone an ambulance.' She whipped a protective shield from her pocket, tore it open and commenced CPR. Anastasia, who led the local branch of the St. John's Ambulance, joined her. Five minutes in, it was apparent the policeman's tracks were not the only thing that was dead in that room. Bombast had shuffled off this mortal coil and sprinted through the gates of hell to join his obnoxious ilk.

Holly, realising she had to do something about the horrifying scene, said, 'Let's give the police and medics room to manoeuvre.' She ushered them all to another room in the shop and, with the help of Anastasia, soon had the customers plied with drinks, from freshly unsealed boxes just in case, and chattering fit to bust.

'Do you think the nasty son of a bitch died of natural causes or was helped through the gates of hades?' Anastasia took a large swig of a fine merlot, shock having her forget her usual sip and savour approach.

Holly did similar and replied, 'I'd bet the bookshop on the fact he was murdered.'

'Who do you think might have done it?'

'Anyone and everyone, apart from the children.' Holly gulped back the merlot as though it was going to save her, and continued, 'If we're going to solve this murder, we'd better keep our wits about us.'

'Wits and drinking wine like it's lemonade don't really go together. Especially when it's you swigging it back.' Then, Anastasia's eyes grew wide as she took in the full extent of Holly's words. 'What do you mean, solve it? That's your beau's job.'

'My bookshop; my investigation.'

Anastasia knew, following a lifetime of friendship, Holly's heels once dug in were well and truly dug, so she might as well go with the flow.

'So, Jane Marple, where do you suggest we start our investigation?' She couldn't help but feel it was a waste of time as no one was really sure there was even a murder, but she was used to indulging her friend.

Any thoughts that Bombast died of natural causes were chucked aside when Danny strode in and announced everyone was to stay exactly where they were. No going home until they were interviewed.

Luckily, Morag had curled up and fallen asleep in her grandmother's lap, so was unaware of the drama going on around her. She should be in her pyjamas, tucked up in bed, not dressed in a party frock in the middle of a murder investigation. Holly felt a wave of love for this beautiful girl who was a bundle of energy, compassion and love all rolled into a tiny package of perfection. How could anyone love a child so much when they were not physically their own? Holly smiled at Danny's mum and stroked Morag's hair back from her forehead. The child stirred, then snuggled back into her gran.

The bookshop owner turned to her bestie and said, 'I'd say murder for sure. Why don't we start with who hated him and would want him dead?'

'Are you having a laugh? We'd be here until next Christmas. Everyone in the county, never mind the village, hated him.'

'Fair point. So, who hated him the most?'

'And is here tonight.' Anastasia poured a glass of wine and handed it over to a customer whose hand was visibly shaking. 'Are you okay, Janet?'

'This death's fair got me rattled.' Janet threw a no-nonsense look at Holly. 'We never had these sorts of o' shenanigans when your grandad owned the bookshop.'

Holly thought this was a tad unfair. They never had anything going on when her grandad was in charge. Not laterally anyway. He'd lost interest in the bookshop and was delighted to hand it over to his granddaughter – lock, stock and several smoking barrels in the crime section. Murder may not have been her intent when she said she would liven things up, but it certainly wasn't her fault it had happened.

'What did you think of Timothy Bombast, Janet?' Holly asked.

'There are actually no words to describe how awful he was.

When they do a post mortem, he'll have vile stamped in the middle.'

'Not a fan then?'

'Not since he sicced Food Standards Scotland on my father's butcher shop.' She glared at Holly. 'The shop just about recovered, but my father never did. It broke him.'

Anastasia looked at Holly and shook her head. Holly said, 'I can understand why you feel so strongly.'

Janet and her merlot headed in the direction of Melissa Nestor, who was now yakking to the local undertaker. Holly wasn't entirely sure why, as his reading tastes tended towards macabre non-fiction. Not once had he purchased a romance book. She wondered if she should speed in their direction and rescue her guest. Then, she decided the guest was perfectly capable of solving her own issues with the help of her assistant and publisher. Holly had bigger fish to fry. In fact, she had a whale sized dead body cluttering up her shop and threatening to ruin her reputation. Even in death Bombast managed to spread vitriol wherever he trod – or, in this case, dropped.

'Why'd you warn me off speaking about Janet's dad?'

'You were in London on a business course when he died. Apparently, it was a massive heart attack and the family blame Timothy's assault on the shop's good name for his early demise.'

'She might be number one on our list then.'

'Yep. And don't forget Curtis.'

'Is he the owner of Cut, Curl and Style?'

'The very one. The hairdresser who had several weeks off with stress is his husband, John.'

'Another perfect motive for murder.'

'There might be numerous motives, but what about alibis?'

'Alibis are a bit of a bear to be honest. We're all alibis for each other.'

'Park alibis for a minute, then, and let's think about means.'

The words were no sooner out of her mouth than Danny appeared in front of her like the ghost of Christmas present. He bent down and whispered in Holly's ear. 'Can I have a quiet word with you?'

Holly indicated he should follow her, and they departed towards her office.

She sat in a chair behind her desk, and he pulled another one up. 'We won't be sure until laboratory analysis comes in, but he was eating a mince pie just prior to his dramatic speech.' He paused, took a deep breath and continued, 'Unfortunately, this makes your mum one of our prime suspects as we think he was poisoned.'

Holly shot to her feet with such force the wheeled office chair shot back and slammed into the filing cabinet. 'How dare you? What makes you think my mother would want to off Timothy Bombast?' She slammed her hands on the desk and leaned forward. 'What possible motive could she have?'

'Your family tried to keep this from you, but the reason your granddad gave up the shop and handed it over to you was because Bombast had it in for him,' Danny said, his voice gentle. 'It was rumoured Timothy Bombast wanted the shop for himself.'

Holly sat down again, all the fight gone from her. 'Why would Bombast want a bookshop? I'll bet he's barely read a book in his life.' Then, her eyes turning icy, she pulled her shoulders back, stood up and marched towards the door. 'I'm going to solve this bally murder and clear my mother's name.'

'Stay out of it, Holly.' In his heart he resigned himself to the fact that there was no way his girlfriend was going to let this drop. To be honest, if it got this case wrapped up before Christmas, he would take every bit of help he could get. The only thing he wanted to be doing in a bookshop was buy his daughter's and Holly's presents. Dead bodies were not a part of his Christmas plans.

Holly took the scenic route around the store; she needed time to think, and it gave her a chance to ogle the main attraction in what was now a crime scene. Gathering her thoughts was also at the forefront of those very thoughts. Being amongst books always calmed her soul and helped her reason more clearly. The current situation required a whole dollop of reasoning if she was going to keep her mother out of the chokey. The tempting aroma of mince pies was at complete odds with the ghoulish sense of doom that hung in the air like an almost palpable cloud. Holly's stomach growled. She regretted not having eaten something before it all kicked off.

She wasn't there for more than a few minutes before being ceremoniously ushered from the room by a polite police officer and a firm grip on her elbow.

She returned to Anastasia, hopping from foot to foot and swigging pinot grigio like it was the elixir of life. 'What's going on?'

'Apparently, they are going to arrest my mother for poisoning the most hated man in the county.' Holly grabbed her friend's glass and took a gulp before handing it back. Getting sloshed wasn't going to help anyone.

'Your mother? The woman who shoos flies out of the window rather than take fly and wasp spray to them?'

'The very one.' She looked around. 'Where is she?'

'Danny took her away.'

'Not to the police station, I hope.' She clunked into a chair, suddenly giddy, pulled her phone from her pocket and pressed speed dial. After a brief conversation she was reassured Noelle was merely being questioned in a different part of the bookshop.

She slumped back, closed her eyes and then leapt to her feet. 'I didn't see the book.'

'What book?' Anastasia looked like a deer in the headlights. There were numerous times where she would love to be able to see inside Holly's brain as it swirled around much faster than hers. Keeping up was a full-time job.

'*The Mysterious Affair at Styles*. First edition. It wasn't on its stand when I went into the front part of the shop.'

'You left a priceless book out in the middle of a party?' The look on Anastasia's face indicated she thought Holly was a few mince pies short of a festivity.

'Book launch. I didn't think anyone would nick it.' Her lip trembled. 'I know everyone who's here.'

'Do you think the missing book and the dead body are related?'

'Who knows?' Exhausted, Holly scrubbed her eyes. She only wanted to do something nice for the village, but it had turned into one unmitigated disaster.

Noelle, newly freed from police interrogation, hurried up to her daughter and enveloped her in a hug. The type only mothers knew how to give.

'What's up? Have they charged you?' Holly said, her words somewhat muffled by her mother's shoulder.

Noelle pulled her back and looked her straight in the eyes. 'They were only asking questions. No one's been arrested.'

Holly's shoulders slumped. 'Grandad's book's disappeared.'

'What book?' Then the light of realisation flashed in her eyes. 'You mean the Agatha Christie?'

Holly sniffled and nodded.

Her mother swallowed. Twice. 'It's only a book. They'll find it.' The look on her face indicated she was aiming for bravery for her daughter's sake. With a final hug, she disappeared to find her husband, leaving Holly with a determination to sort out their current problems. Problems being a tad understated.

She turned back to Anastasia, pulled her shoulders back and said, 'We're going to find that book and get to the bottom of this murder.'

'I like your enthusiasm, and I applaud it. How do you suggest we do so?'

'First, we'll write that list of the key suspects. Then we're going to ask everyone here who they think did it.'

'What? They're hardly going to spill.'

'Oh, they'll spill. It's gossip city here right now.' She smiled, the first genuine one since the event began. 'This is the perfect time to do it.'

'You're evil.' Anastasia threw back her head and laughed, garnering looks from all corners of the room. It lightened the mood, and the chatter seemed freer.

'Ready, steady, go talk scandal.' True to her word, Holly swivelled and headed towards the crowds.

Curtis was in the mood for gossip, and then some. 'The intolerable pig deserved to die. Someone's done the world a favour.'

'How's John?'

'Couldn't face coming tonight because he knew the pig would be here. He's probably celebrating now I've told him he's been murdered.'

Interesting. I wonder if he sneaked in here somehow and poisoned the mince pies.

'Who do you think did it?'

'Could have been anyone in the room.' He frowned. If you're opening a book on the murderer, I'd actually say the local bookie.'

'Kent? Why on earth would he want to kill Timothy Bombast?' He appeared to be one of the few people Bombast hadn't upset.

'Our bookie has been a bit too liberal with the betting himself and his business was about to go down the tubes. The pig was blackmailing him.'

'Blackmail? I thought our victim was more the publish and be damned type.'

'Branching out, apparently. Must go, darling. Mingling calls.

Need to schmooze all those with hair like rats' tails.' He pushed his own perfect locks back off his forehead as he strolled off, looking as if he did not have a care in the world.

Gossipmongering calls more like. Holly strolled towards Kent in as nonchalant a manner as she could muster. Given the gravity of the situation, it was difficult. 'Kent. Good to see you here. We don't often see you treading the aisles amongst book-shelves.'

'I'm here to get the wife's Christmas present. She's up North staying with her mother, so I took the opportunity to get a signed copy of the bilge she reads.'

'Melissa Nestor's work is highly regarded.' Holly frowned. 'New York Times Best Seller and won a gazillion awards.'

'Aye. Lassies like that sort of thing.'

Holly had had enough of his chauvinistic attitude. 'How's the bookie business going? I've heard times are hard.'

'Who told you that?' He took a step forward, his hands hovering in the vicinity of Holly's throat.

Holly took a step back but said, quite bravely given the dead body already cluttering the place up, 'Touch me and I'll be prac-ticing my karate skills on you.' Holly had never been to a karate class in her life, but her words hit harder than any furi zuki could. She had read a book on karate once, and surely that counted. She waited until his hands dropped and he adopted a hangdog expression. 'Times are tough, then?'

To be honest, she wondered how anyone could have a tough time running a bookies. They usually made out like bandits, although that might be a rather unfortunate description given what they did.

He tried for bravado via bluster but settled on desperation. 'I've got a temporary cash flow issue, but it will be solved soon.'

'Solved how?'

This time, bravado won. 'What's it got to do with you?'

'Considering I've a dead body mingling with the Christmas decorations, I'd say it had everything to do with me.' She crossed her arms. 'Does your sudden solvency have anything to do with said body no longer blackmailing you?'

'What? How?...'

'Time to fess up. What was he blackmailing you about?'

He sighed. 'He said he had evidence I was laundering money.' More heavy sighing. 'I barely have a halfpenny to rub together, never mind launder. He was making the whole blasted thing up. That wouldn't stop him ruining my reputation, though.'

'Still, you've got a perfect reason to kill him.'

'And the perfect alibi. I've been speaking to someone since I arrived.'

'And the solvency?'

'I'm not sure it's got anything to do with you, Miss Nosy Parker, but my great uncle died, and he's left me a tidy sum in his will.'

Not likely to be him then. If he's telling the truth, of course. She made a note to let Danny know all this the minute she was allowed anywhere near him. She wasn't sure what to do with this dead end. She pointed him in the direction of the drinks table and then headed in the direction of another victim to interrogate.

Interrogation gave her nothing more than a headache and a feeling she was no further forward. One thing was established – every person in the village had a motive for killing the reporter, including Holly herself. So, motive wasn't going to get them anywhere. Means was a bit trickier to establish and opportunity again left the field wide open. The only people she hadn't chatted to were Nestor and her publisher, but they were under public scrutiny every minute, being the guests of honour. Even amid tragedy they continued to schmooze, delightfully in the case of Melissa and smarmily in the case of her publisher. Something tickled at the back of her brain re the publisher. Hadn't she heard something about them recently? Something not at the esteemed end of the publishing spectrum. She hurried in the direction of Anastasia. On the way she accosted Danny. 'My grandad's first edition Agatha Christie is missing. Can you get your guys to ask around?'

'I'm in the middle of a murder investigation. Priorities.'

'See here, Mr Tetchy, the two cases could be linked.' She put her arms on her hips and glared at him.

'Stop with the attitude. Remember, you're also a suspect.' He glared back at her, then, taking in the look on her face, he added, 'I'll see what I can do.' He laid a comforting hand on her arm.

She mustered up her best smile, which, although still rather on the weak side, was better than the abject misery squeezing her heart. *How could my first major event in a bookshop go so wrong?*

She had two mysteries to solve and, quite frankly, she wasn't sure which one was more upsetting. She weighed it up and decided, on balance, she was more upset about the book. The only part of Bombast's death that upset her was that he was cluttering up the main part of her bookshop and had ruined a perfectly planned and highly anticipated launch. Other than that, he was no loss to the world. She did momentarily wonder if anyone would miss him and then dismissed the thought. Bombast was vocal in stating he ploughed a lone furrow. No one to shackle him were his own words. Holly strongly suspected the real reason was no sane person could bear him, as the only person he really loved was himself. She shook herself out of her reverie, squared her shoulders and prepared for another round of questioning. Discussing stolen books and murder was not how she envisioned spending her evening, far less interrogating ninety percent of her customers, half the village, and a high-profile publisher. If she'd known bookshop owning was a high-octane sport, she might have sold up rather than titivating and relaunching her inheritance.

She spotted Anastasia at the other end of the shop. Her

dazzling smile appeared to be charming everyone to whom she spoke. It never failed; she'd been using that smile to good effect since they'd met at nursery. It carried her all the way through school and now to make her the fastest growing and most respected sommelier in the country. Hard work was also involved but that smile won the most hardened of hearts over. Except for their corpse, of course. Winning over and Timothy Bombast would never belong in the same sentence. Then fear clutched at Holly's heart as she realised Anastasia could be their murderer. She had motive – Timothy Bombast had written a scathing review of her business in the local paper – and she had opportunity. As well as setting out the wine, her friend also set out the mince pies. Unsupervised. Surely not. The article had barely made a dent in her ascending star, so murdering the journalist was hardly worth a life sentence and the tarnishing of a thriving business. She shoved the thought aside, but it continued to tickle at her cerebral cortex, flinging another dark cloud in her general direction.

Worrying would get them nowhere; action would get them, if not somewhere, at least further along the road to solving the two mysteries tarnishing her lavish opening. Christmasy it was not. Nor was it cheery. So, Christmas cheer had flown right out of the window. Deciding a book hunt would be more manageable than a murder hunt, she organised a group of guests, who were only too happy to help. She noted several of them had piles of books beside them and hoped against hope they were planning on buying them all. Boredom had set in, so she soon had several volunteers.

'Keep out of the way of the police.' She also gave them a description of said book and showed them a photo on her mobile phone.

With murmurs of assent, they dispersed. One was heard to mutter, 'Books in bookshops and needles in haystacks spring to mind.'

She couldn't help but feel they had a point.

Grilling Anastasia as to how much she'd learned from the assembled masses elicited, 'Apart from how universally hated he was, zilch. Even his aunt said his mother had emigrated to get away from him.'

Her heart sank. 'So, everyone is a suspect.'

'I did hear one interesting thing, though. A couple of your more voracious readers keep up with all the industry news. They take readaholic into the stratosphere.'

'Thank the good lord. They keep my till ringing and my doors open.'

'It also means they know everything about everything and everyone when it comes to books.' She paused, a smirk on her face.

'Spit it out. I'd like this fiasco to be over so my till can start ringing again and we can all go home.'

'Rumour has it our esteemed guest is looking at changing publishers. If this happens the publisher who is standing next to her now is going to go bust.'

Holly wasn't in the mood for rumours. 'Aren't there contracts or something. She can't just swan off into the sunset arm in arm with a new publisher.'

'Apparently, the bigger Melissa Nestor got, the better her contract got. It would appear Melissa is not as airheaded as her books would suggest. Word on the street is she has a savvy business head on her shoulder.'

'Killing Timothy Bombast wouldn't help with that.'

'True. It's interesting, though.'

Her thoughts were leaning towards John, the hairdresser. What's the betting he said he wasn't up to the launch party, so they didn't suspect him. They used all sorts in hairdresser shops. She hurried towards Danny to enlighten him with her blinding insights. He thanked her but seemed less than enthused. 'We've to look into all possibilities, starting with the people who are actually here.' He turned back to his colleague.

By this point, Holly was at a bit of a loss. Her investigation was staler than a Christmas cake in July. Despite the fact the local reporter was now decorating her flooring, she was sure the press would pick up on this and her business would be plastered across the front of every newspaper in the country. She dropped into the nearest chair like the heroine in one of Nestor's books.

'Are you okay?' Danny was bending over her, concern shining from his gorgeous eyes. She now definitely felt like one of Nestor's heroines, complete with fluttering heart. Not that she'd read a Nestor book, but her mother had told her everything she needed to know. Every time a new book came out, she gave Holly a blow-by-blow account. Holly could probably pass muster on Mastermind with her specialist subject being Melissa Nestor Romance Novels.

She went to check on Morag who was still fast asleep in her grandmother's arms, blissfully unaware of the drama swirling around her. 'If you need a break, lay her on the couch and I'll find a blanket from the Children's area.'

'That would be great. I could do with a drink and moving around a bit.'

Holly called Parvati Singh over. The young girl had babysat Morag numerous times to allow Holly and Danny to go out. A voracious reader, she was off to study English Literature at Oxford, and the babysitting money was being squirreled away to supplement her grant money. Her parents bought her any books she wanted and always had done.

Morag murmured when she was moved but settled back into sleep immediately. Holly covered her with a Peppa Pig blanket, which Anastasia had fetched. Holly hoped one day she would be this child's mother. How she could feel so much love for a child that was not her own was a mystery to her, but a mystery she fully welcomed and embraced. Not like the mystery of the dead body stuffed between her bookshelves or the mystery of the missing book. Would they ever be solved and would this bally book launch ever go ahead? Ordinarily, she'd be more worried about the fact someone had lost their life but the only feeling she had about Bombast's death was relief. She strongly suspected the whole room felt the same.

Hearing the doors go and a kerfuffle at the crime scene, she jumped up and hurried over. Danny was watching two men as they zipped it into a body bag, loaded it onto a trolley and took it away. Nausea swept over her. Never in her worst nightmares did she imagine running a bookshop would be anything like this. She'd given up a high-powered city job, and now it looked like her new business was about to fold. Dead bodies cluttering the place up and holding your customers hostage whilst they waited to be interrogated by the police was not a good look.

Loud voices broke her reverie. She supposed it was inevitable given the time everyone had been cooped up. They were probably all at the stage where they'd be willing to commit their own murder if it meant they'd get through the front door of the bookshop. She was surprised no one had murdered Danny.

The local minister, Darren Letham, stood with his hands up in front of him in a gesture of peace. Stephen Tiernan was giving it big licks, as the locals would say. 'You' blithering idiot. Look at the state of my suit.' Spittle sprayed across the minister's face.

As becomes a man of the cloth, Sarren calmly wiped the spittle from his face and said, 'Sorry. I'll pay for it to be dry cleaned.'

'This is Armani. You will buy a new one.' His pointed finger landed mere millimetres from Darren's face.

Darren put his hands down and curled them at his side. 'No use making a fuss here. We'll discuss it in a minute away from everyone. Why don't you go and find some napkins to mop the worst of it up?'

The publisher stomped off, a scowl on his face.

Darren turned towards Kirsty, pulled something from under his jacket and handed it over.

She stared at the item in her hand, and her brows shot up. 'What...? How...?' She held her first edition of *The Mysterious Affair at Styles*. 'Where did you find it?'

'Tucked inside our publisher's jacket. The commotion was so I could transfer it back to its rightful owner.'

'How on earth...' She wasn't even sure how to continue. 'Where did you learn that? It's not exactly the magic trick a vicar usually performs?'

'Minister, my dear, we are in Scotland.'

'Minister. Vicar. Whatever. How did you manage it and where did you learn it?'

'Learned it in the family business. I'm a bad boy turned good. I found God while I was doing porridge and have been on the straight and narrow since.' He grinned. 'Until tonight, of course. It was good to know I still had it.' He took in the look on Kirsty's face. 'Not that I'm going to use it again.'

'I should jolly well hope not, Reverend.' A twinkle appeared in Kirsty's eyes before they turned belligerent. 'Wait until I get my hands on him. She turned to go but was stopped in her tracks by a gentle hand and soft tone.

'Not so fast. I've more news.'

She turned to face him and said, 'Go on. I'm always up for a spot of gossip.'

'When I saw the bulge in Tiernan's jacket, I did a bit of digging online.' Forestalling Kirsty's question, he added, 'Better not to ask.'

She shook her head but merely said, 'Carry on.'

Stephen Tiernan is a bad boy made not so good. He was a rising star in the publishing world but fell from grace spectacularly amidst rumours of fraud. Nothing that could be proved, but still.' He paused as if for dramatic effect. 'His current company is knee deep in debt and scandal. Our corpse was about to write an explosive article that would make the whole house of cards come tumbling down. His whole life is nothing but smoke and mirrors.'

'Good grief. So, he stole my book to get himself out of debt.'

'Precisely. No idea if he killed Bombast but I wouldn't put it past him.'

'I'm off to give him what for.' Her dander was well and truly up. She didn't care how much trouble his business was in; he wasn't getting away with trying to ruin hers. He could crawl out of his hole somewhere else.

'Wait... he could be dangerous.'

'I don't care.'

She marched right up to Bombast. 'How dare you?'

'What are you talking about? This whole affair has been a shambles. I am going to bring your pathetic excuse of a bookshop down.'

Melissa Nestor stepped in. 'That's quite enough.'

He pushed her aside and continued his tirade on Kirsty. 'You do not know what I can do to you.'

'Something worse than stealing my grandad's first edition Agatha Christie?'

The publisher patted his coat and turned white.

'You miserable excuse of a human being. I'm going to bring you down.'

'Just like you brought your own business down. It's worthless.' Kirsty couldn't believe she was saying these things. 'And now you're facing charges for theft.'

Before she could say dumb move Kirsty, she found herself in a chokehold with a knife at her throat. Tiernan seemed to be a master at concealing things on his person.

'Stephen, stop this.' Melissa's voice had taken on a high pitch, a change from her usual soft tones.

'This is all your fault you stupid bitch,' he spat out. 'You're leaving the company. Back off or I'll slit her throat.'

Melissa did as requested, a look of horror on her face.

Danny appeared in the room and stopped dead when he saw what was going on.

Tiernan turned his attention back to Kirsty. 'Why couldn't you mind your own business? The last person to interfere in my affairs has just left in a body bag.' His grin was less jolly, ho, ho, ho and more chilling, someone is going to die. 'The size of him I knew he'd be shovelling down mince pies like they were medicine. A spot of poison, hand him a plate and Bombast's a goner.'

Danny took a tentative step forward. He kept his voice calm as he said, 'Let her go and we can talk about this.'

'No talking. I've nothing to lose by bumping her off as well.'

Before Danny could get another word out of his mouth, Stephen Tiernan went limp and fell to the floor amidst glass and an expensive merlot which spread rapidly over the laminate.

Kirsty was too relieved to care about whether the flooring was ruined. By the look of the gash on his head there was probably blood in the mix, so there would be a professional clean up anyway. Kirsty's mother stood with the neck of the merlot bottle in her hand, eyes wide. 'Am I going to be arrested for assault?' She thought for a minute and added, a tremble in her voice, or murder.'

Danny moved over to her. 'No. You're more likely to get a medal for bravery.'

Kirsty flew into her mother's arms and hugged her as if she would never let go. Then, actually letting go, she said to Danny, 'Once he's been carted off to hospital, in handcuffs I hope, can we get back to what festivities are left.'

'Seeing as he's admitted murder and there's a hundred witnesses to assault and your attempted murder, I would say so.' He looked at the floor. 'Just keep everyone away from here.

In the end, the launch could be deemed a success. The till rang and rang and rang as guests bought *Snow-Tinged Love* and many other books in every possible colour and genre. This would be one book launch that would never be forgotten. Melissa asked if it would be all right if she held the launch of her first romantic suspense novel at the shop. It would be coming out in time for Easter. 'As a way of apology for the unmitigated disaster that was my current publisher. I can assure you the next publisher is much saner.'

Kirsty accepted. She ushered the last customer out the door around midnight. She looked around and decided to open an hour later in the morning to finish tidying up.

Who knew bookshops could be murder? She jolly well hoped there wasn't this level of excitement in the future.

BIO:

Wendy H. Jones is a multi-award-winning, best-selling Scottish author of crime thrillers, cozy mysteries, children's picture books and non-fiction books for authors. She won the Books Go Social Book of the Year at Dublin writers conference and the prestigious Scottish Association of Writers, Janetta Bowie Chalice for best non-fiction book She is also an acclaimed international public speaker teaching writing craft and marketing worldwide. In addition, she is the Editor in Chief of Writers' Narrative eMagazine, a partner in Auscot Publishing and Retreats and owner of Scott and Lawson Publishing.

https://www.wendyhjones.com

Chapter Two

TIDINGS OF TERROR

Marti M. McNair

I n the town of Hollybrook, a shadow took form,
an unsettling presence, a brewing storm.
But the children stepped forward, their faces aglow,
The nativity story, they wanted all to know,
Yet something felt twisted, and not quite right,
And tension arose on that Christmas Eve night.
And when the last carol was set to be sung,
The atmosphere thickened, and a heaviness hung.
For Elwin was missing, his seat cold and bare
No musical notes, left an air of despair.

In the village of Hollybrook, Christmas Eve was sacred. It was a night when the townsfolk gathered in the little stone church in the heart of the village, their voices filling the snow-covered town with the sound of familiar carols. Soft candlelight bathed the faces of old and young alike, each bundled against the cold, singing in unison, along with the organ's rich tones.

But this year, an uneasy feeling settled in Mary Fulton's gut, refusing to let go. For fifteen years, she had led the choir with a sharp ear for perfection, and Christmas Eve in Hollybrook was her moment of triumph. Yet today, a shadow loomed over the festivities, one embodied by Elwin Crawford, the church organist. When she greeted him earlier, he had brushed her off, eyed her suspiciously, and looked as if the weight of the world sat on his shoulders.

Not only that, but Mary's acute ears caught the subtle discord in Elwin's playing; a few notes slipped from their intended path, creating a jarring contrast against the otherwise harmonious melody in the first song. Each misplayed chord stood out, grating against her finely tuned sensibilities. This was extremely unusual for Elwin.

As the last notes of "Silent Night" faded, Mary gazed out of one of the large stained glass windows. For a moment, she thought she caught a glimpse of movement - was it a person? She squinted, pressing her face against the glass until her breath clouded its surface. Who could it be? Her mind raced through the possibilities: a lost traveller, perhaps. Had someone come to disrupt the peace of Christmas Eve? Just as she began to focus, the figure vanished into the night.

Mabel Collins ushered the children eagerly to the makeshift stage, her voice alive with excitement. 'And now, dear friends of Hollybrook, we have a delightful treat for you this evening. The Sunday school children are thrilled to present their nativity performance.'

Mary's attention returned to the service, momentarily casting aside her unease. Tiny shepherds, wrapped in flowing white sheets, and angels draped in shimmering tinsel eagerly took their places, filling the space with innocent energy. They tiptoed across the creaky platform, their small voices weaving the nativity story with wonder-filled expressions.

As the play concluded, parents rose from their pews, hearts swelling with pride as they erupted into applause, cheers of delight echoing through the church. Mary wiped away tears of joy, while others exchanged gleeful glances. Mary looked up at Elwin in his organ loft. He sat on his bench with a solemn expression, his brow furrowed and lips pressed tightly together. Usually, Elwin would be at the forefront of the clapping, setting the rhythm for the rest of the congregation.

Minister Brodie shuffled his way to the pulpit to give his thanks. After a short prayer, he said, 'And now, we will close with our last carol of the evening. Please, be upstanding and join in singing together, "O' Come, All Ye Faithful".'

The congregation shifted, ready to lift their voices in song, but when the introduction from the organ failed to sound, a ripple of confusion swept through the crowd. Murmurs of uncertainty could be heard from all corners as heads turned upwards to the organ loft, searching for Elwin Crawford. Where could he be?

Mary's brow furrowed, her earlier sense of unease returning.

For Elwin, playing the organ was everything, it was as if the instrument was a part of himself and as unshakable as the church's stone walls. Yet here it stood, alone, without Elwin's fingers dancing across its keys.

Minister Brodie cleared his throat. 'Friends,' he began, raising his hand to quieten the restless crowd. 'I'm sure Elwin has just popped out and will return. However, in his absence, let us close our evening with another prayer.' He bowed his head, and the congregation followed suit.

With the final *amen*, those gathered slowly rose, boots shuffling against the stone-tiled floor, coats pulled tight against the chill. One by one, they filed out into the gravelled churchyard. Outside, the world was shrouded in twilight and silence, the moon casting a spectral glow on the snow-draped trees.

As the congregation disappeared into the snowy night, Mary's pulse quickened. Elwin was nowhere to be found, and an image of the shadowy figure lurking in the graveyard crept into her mind, tugging at her sense of dismay. She moved through the empty church, her footsteps echoing in the stillness. 'Elwin.' She called his name softly, her voice swallowed by the thick silence that clung to every pew and every hymn book.

In the back vestry, she paused, noticing Elwin's woollen scarf and jacket hanging neatly on his hook. Mary moved down the narrow hallway to the small room below the organ loft, where Elwin would often slip away for a few moments of quiet before the service. But the door creaked open to an empty space. Mary couldn't help but feel Elwin's sudden absence was no ordinary mystery – something was amiss within Hollybrook's walls tonight.

By morning, Hollybrook was abuzz with speculation, the hum of rumours thickening the frosty air. Elwin Crawford was nowhere to be found – no sign of him at home, no note on his door, and nothing to explain his vanishing.

In the bustling kitchen of the community centre, winter sunlight streamed through the frosted windows, casting a warm glow over the lively preparations of the Holiday Hope and Meals programme, organised by the Church Elders. The aroma of simmering herbs and freshly chopped vegetables filled the bustling room as volunteers moved around, preparing Christmas dinner for the homeless and housebound.

Jenny Bishop stood over a large steaming pot, carefully stirring fragrant chicken broth with a sturdy wooden spoon. 'If I hadn't arrived late for the service,' she began, her expression thoughtful as she looked up. 'I might never have seen him – whoever it was, wandering around the headstones.' She paused, adding salt and pepper to the soup. 'He looked . . . uneasy, but was making sure he'd be seen. When I got closer, he made a run for it, waving a baseball bat. Do you think it could have been Elwin? He has been acting strange recently.'

Mary, standing just a few steps away at the counter, halted mid-chop, her knife hovering above the half-diced carrots on the cutting board. She looked over at Jenny, her brows knitting. 'At what point in the service did you come in?

Jenny, still stirring the pot, seemed to search her memory. 'It was just after "Silent Night",' she said, as if reliving the moment. 'The children had just taken their places for the nativity.'

Mary shook her head, her brow creasing. 'It couldn't have been Elwin. He was still inside and on his bench after the nativity ended. He must have slipped out as Minister Brodie gave his thanks and prayed.' She paused, chewing her bottom lip. 'I thought I caught a glimpse of someone moving outside, but I brushed it off, thinking it was just shadows playing tricks.' She met Jenny's gaze. 'But what if someone was wandering around out there . . . and Elwin left to meet them?'

Ella Williamson piped up. 'Was he having money problems? Because I saw him outside the payday lenders in the next town, not long ago. I just thought, with Christmas coming up, he might need a few pounds to get by. You know how tight things can be at this time of year. It wouldn't surprise me if he was feeling the pinch.' She glanced around at the others, her expression full of concern.

Nancy Brown, cheeks flushed, cleared her throat into her sleeve. 'As far as I know, Elwin's loaded. His parents left him their house down south, and he sold it for a killing and moved up here. There were no other siblings, so he inherited it all.' She paused, her voice trailing off as if reluctance crept in. 'Elwin . . . he met a woman - a person he thought he could share his life with. They found each other on a social media group - something to do with music.'

Mary blinked, then let out a surprised chuckle. 'And Elwin told you all this?'

Nancy nodded. 'It was me who helped him set all his social media up, so he kind of confided in me as the romance progressed. I don't know too much, other than she approached him, they swapped phone numbers, and before you know it, they're dating. If it all worked out, he was going to bring her to church to meet us all. But he promised me to secrecy until then.'

Gasps rippled through the small crowd, and a few shook their heads in disbelief. Lucy Hamilton glanced over her shoulder. 'If it wasn't that lover haunting him, it was family trouble,' she said, her tone grave. 'A relative of his, with a reputation that's . . . not nice - so Elwin said. They turned up a few weeks back, unannounced and have been hovering about like a bad smell. Elwin didn't say too much, other than he was at his wits end with him.'

Maggie Deans, her hands deep in soapy water as she scrubbed pots, glanced up. 'You know, other than at church, the last time I saw Elwin was a few weeks ago at the train station in the city.' She said, her voice mirroring the puzzlement on her expression. 'I was just getting back from down south when I bumped square into him on the platform. I said, "Fancy meeting you here", but he just looked right through me, like I was invisible. Then, out of nowhere, he smiled, tipped his head in that way he does, and walked past me without a word. It felt so strange - as if he were there and not there at the same time.'

The gossiping grew, each theory feeding off the others, spreading like flames in an inferno. In the mists of the simmering pots and chopped vegetables, the atmosphere shifted, filling the kitchen with a tension thicker than the steam hanging in the air. A single, gnawing question remained – what had happened to Elwin Crawford?

Later that evening, Mary, Jenny and Minister Brodie came together around a long, festively arranged table in Mary's dining room. The golden-brown turkey took pride of place at the centre, flanked by a colourful array of trimmings, roast potatoes infused with rosemary, buttery carrots and a luscious, rich gravy, promising to elevate every bite.

'I'm really worried about Elwin,' Mary said, dabbing her mouth with a napkin. 'There's so much speculation swirling around, and the police don't seem to be making any progress.'

Minister Brodie nodded thoughtfully, his expression grave. 'It's so strange that nobody saw or heard him leave. He may have slipped out, but surely someone must have noticed something.'

As Mary gathered their plates, the soft clatter of china echoed through the room as she made her way to the kitchen. Jenny raised her voice to carry over the distance. 'I told the police about the figure in the graveyard - the one who was waving the baseball bat.' She shook her head. 'But I haven't heard anything since. Not a word.'

Mary reappeared, balancing a magnificent trifle in her arms. The dessert sparkled with a display of colours, its layers of delicate sponge, velvety cream, and plump fruit creating an inviting image that beckoned eager spoons. As they indulged in the last mouthfuls, the richness of the trifle left them content and smiling. Leaning back, they sipped steaming cups of coffee and ate after-dinner mints.

'Do you think we should pop along to the church and do some searching for ourselves?' Mary asked, pouring sherry into three crystal glasses. 'We might find clues about Elwin's disappearance in his music sheets or find something in the small room where he often hung out.'

The enchanting beauty of Hollybrook unfolded before them - a winter wonderland bathed in moonlight, where tiny stars twinkled against the velvet sky. It illuminated the snow-draped rooftops and brightened the shimmering icicles that hung from the eaves. Yet, amidst the charm and serenity, a cloud of mystery darkened the festive spirit.

Their footfalls crunched over the snow-laden path, their steps leaving a crisp imprint in the powdery white blanket. As they moved along, their tracks formed a winding trail behind them until they reached the church.

Minister Brodie put the key in the lock and, gripping the heavy iron handle, he pulled hard. The large oak doors creaked open to reveal the shadowed interior, greeting them with the faint scent of candle wax and old wood.

They spread out across the dimly lit space, the floorboards creaking as they went. Mary took a deep breath, steeling herself as she moved towards the pews, heading for the stairs leading to the organ loft. Reaching Elwin's bench, she paused, noticing a stack of music sheets dumped on the floor.

Picking them up, she brushed her fingers over the pages, their edges frayed from use. Some were covered in Elwin's own pencilled symbols and musical notes. The sight was like a ghostly fingerprint, a piece of Elwin left behind. When Mary flipped to the sheet titled "God Rest Ye' Merry Gentlemen", her eyes caught something unusual. A message was written in the margins, printed in Elwin's tight, careful script. '*My favourite place for contemplation - where the bells never ring.*' Slightly below it, this time in a hurried, almost frantic scribble, were the words, '*My biggest regret - not knowing what happened to Lydia. Never hearing her beautiful voice in song again.'*

'Lydia?' Mary whispered, racking her brain. There hadn't been a Lydia in the choir, not in all the years she had led it. She searched her memory, feeling the familiar pull of faces and names, but no one called Lydia had ever sung in their small, tight-knit group. A shiver prickled her skin - whoever this Lydia was, she had haunted Elwin's thoughts enough to slip into the margins of his music, his last cryptic words scrawled in haste. Had he been thinking of her when he played that final hymn? As his hands moved over the keys, was his mind somewhere distant? Was that why some of the chords sounded off?

Mary descended the stairs back to the body of the church, where Jenny and Minister Brodie waited. 'Who is Lydia?' she asked, handing Minister Brodie the music sheet.

His expression became subdued. 'Lydia was . . . someone Elwin cared about deeply,' he said, his voice sounding emotional. 'She was from his home village, and according to Elwin, she vanished without a trace. It nearly destroyed him. After his parents passed away, he moved up here, hoping to start anew and leave the past behind. He loved the people of Hollybrook for welcoming him and making him feel part of our community. Together, we helped him move on.'

Jenny nodded, her gaze fixed on a distant point, a memory stirring in her eyes. 'I remember Elwin when he first arrived in town. He was a poor soul with a broken heart. He said he would tell me the story of Lydia when he felt up to it, but never did. It must have been too painful, so he closed the memory off and didn't mention her again. Not to me, anyway.'

Mary's breath hitched. 'Do you think whatever happened to Lydia all those years ago has something to do with Elwin going missing now?'

Minister Brodie's gaze fell to the music sheet in his hand. 'It's hard to say, Mary, but . . . I don't think Elwin ever truly let go of Lydia. She still held a place in his heart as he never pursued another love interest. Perhaps he left, looking for answers that he couldn't find all those years ago?'

'But it doesn't make any sense,' Mary replied, with a sigh. 'According to Nancy Brown, he just met someone on a social media site. Why didn't he wait until after the service to leave, and why didn't he tell anyone where he was going?'

Jenny shivered, her eyes darting from Minister Brodie to Mary. 'You know how Elwin was. He held onto things, people, and perhaps, even though he never mentioned it, to the past. If he believed he could find her or solve whatever happened to her, there's nothing he wouldn't risk.' She swallowed, her voice a thin whisper. 'Perhaps it's the past that's finally come calling.'

'Why am I only learning of all this now?' Mary asked.

Minister Brodie adjusted his glasses, pushing them firmly up the bridge of his nose. 'You moved to Hollybrook much later than Elwin, and as Jenny has said, Elwin never discussed the matter.'

As the conversation deepened, a tight knot formed in Mary's stomach. 'We need to find out what happened to Lydia.' It was almost as if the weight of history was pressing against her. 'I think if we solve that puzzle, it will be the answer to finding Elwin.'

Jenny's expression brightened. 'If Elwin was searching for her, there might be clues hidden in the town, places he frequented, or people he spoke to. We can't let this pass without checking.'

Minister Brodie sighed. 'Then we must act quickly. The longer we wait, the more we risk losing what little we know. Let's try to uncover the truth, not just for Elwin, but for Lydia too. We may need to visit Elwin's birth town. I'll check the train timetables and book three tickets.'

As they prepared to leave, Mary glanced back at the organ loft and the abandoned sheets of music that seemed to hold secrets. With one last look, she turned and stepped into the crisp, cold night, determined to follow wherever their search would lead them - hopefully to reveal the truth of Lydia's fate and restore peace to both souls.

Mary began her quiet interrogation of the choir members at the Boxing Day singalong. Speaking to each one in turn, she hoped to catch a flicker of hidden knowledge. Most of them had been singing at the church for many years and were close to Elwin.

Taking a deep breath, Mary approached Hilda Adams, the church's eldest member. Hilda sat quietly in her familiar seat, her silver hair neatly pinned back and her gnarled hands resting on her lap. 'I'm trying to understand what's happened to Elwin,' Mary said, keeping her voice low. 'Did he ever mention a love interest called Lydia or the possibility of a new romance?'

Hilda's eyes, usually bright and lively, clouded with concern. She glanced at her lap, her fingers fidgeting. 'Oh, Lydia . . . she was the love of Elwin's life. I don't think he would ever have room in his heart for anyone else. He was troubled when he came to Hollybrook, but I don't think it was just Lydia who worried him. I think there are more family secrets in his closet than in a gossip column on a rainy Monday morning.

'What family secrets do you think he's hiding?' Mary asked.

Hilda shuddered, her expression turning sour. 'His brother, for one. When Elwin first arrived in Hollybrook, he rented a room from me. Within weeks, Arthur showed up looking for him. Elwin chased him off, declaring he was nothing but a bad egg. He'd been in trouble that led to imprisonment. and Elwin made me promise not to tell anyone about him. But that was so many years ago now.'

'I thought Elwin was an only child. After his parents died, he was the sole inheritor of their estate.' Mary said, contemplating what she had heard previously, and comparing it to what Hilda revealed.

'I think that's what Elwin wanted people to believe,' Hilda replied. 'But I can assure you, he has - or had - a brother. I used to walk my spaniel, Queenie, through the old church grounds - past the bell tower. That was the last time I saw Arthur. He was there, arguing with Elwin.'

A chill settled over Mary as Hilda's words sank in. She thought of the music sheet she had passed to Minister Brodie. Elwin's writing had referred to bells that had never rung. Could he have been hinting at something amiss at the old bell tower?

Hilda leaned in, her voice a murmur. 'I saw the police poking about the graveyard this morning. Betty Harper's husband was the leading officer, and she says they found nothing awry. Not a trace of anything odd. Seems to me it was likely just some mischief-maker out for a bit of a holiday larking, if you ask me.'

Next, Mary sought out Henry Perkins, the church's groundskeeper, a quiet man rarely given to sharing tales. But this time, he leaned close to Mary, delighted to share his thoughts. 'For many Christmases, I'd glimpse a shadowy figure slipping through the graveyard. I just put it down to a youngster playing pranks. However, now that Elwin is missing, I'm wondering if it's been Lydia visiting all along. Trying to entice Elwin to pack up and leave for wherever it is she's gone. She was the love of his life. So, if that's the case, I hope he's found happiness.'

'What can you tell me about the old grounds of the church, out past the bell tower?' Mary asked.

'I cut the grass in spring and summer and tend to the weeding. Hardly anyone visits,' Henry said. 'The gravestones are ancient, with no living relatives around to tend to them. If it wasn't for the fact it was a graveyard, the council would have scooped it up for housing by now.'

That evening, Mary returned to the manse to meet with Minister Brodie and Jenny. The warm amber light spilled from the windows into the frosty night, casting a welcoming glow as she rattled the door. 'It's just me,' she called, as she stepped inside.

In the lounge, the open coal fire crackled, its orange flames flickering shadows across the walls. The smell of woodsmoke mixed with the scent of hot chocolate and gingerbread filled the room with a festive warmth. Mary breathed in the comforting aroma as she settled into a chair, and Jenny gestured to a steaming mug on the table. 'That one's yours,' Jenny said, smiling. 'It's fresh, and there's cake, too - help yourself.'

As Mary savoured a generous bite of gingerbread slathered with butter, Minister Brodie and Jenny listened intently to all Mary had learned. They nodded along, absorbing each detail as she recounted her discoveries.

'We looked through all Elwin's music today, and you won't believe what we found in the carol sheets,' Jenny began, glancing between Minister Brodie and Mary. 'Each sheet seems to hold secret messages. We've taken notes, but one stood out - The Holly and the Ivy.'

Mary's eyes widened. 'What did you find?'

Jenny held the sheet to Mary and pointed to the handwriting above. 'Seek the ivy where the holly cannot grow, beneath stone and shadow, the truth will show. As much as other sheets had small cryptic messages, this one was the longest.'

Mary frowned, reading it to herself. 'What does it all mean?'

Minister Brodie's face turned thoughtful. 'Ivy thrives in shade, especially where other plants struggle. Could Elwin be directing us to a specific spot outside the church, somewhere shadowed?'

'Of course!' Mary said, slapping her forehead, the realisation hitting her immediately. 'The ivy-covered headstones by the old bell tower. It's the oldest part of the church grounds. I think this place held significance to Elwin.'

Jenny's face lit up, and nodding eagerly, she said, 'Those must be the same bells Elwin wrote about, the ones that never ring. They've been silent for centuries.'

Minister Brodie leaned forward, his eyes sparkling. 'And to reach that part of the grounds you have to pass right through the graveyard beside the church.' He paused as if imagining the actual path to the bell tower. He turned to Jenny, perhaps the person you saw lurking on Christmas Eve wasn't lingering in the graveyard at all, but was on their way toward the old cemetery.'

Mary nodded thoughtfully. 'Hilda mentioned the police didn't spot anything suspicious at the graveyard. But I bet they didn't even think to look around the old grounds by the bell tower. How do you fancy a nice early morning walk? I'll meet you at the cemetery at eight sharp.'

Mary, Minister Brodie, and Jenny stepped into the old grounds, the world around them peaceful and still as if time itself had drifted away. The bell tower loomed ahead, its once proud stones crumbling and withered, draped in a thin veil of snow. Its steeple rose jaggedly, etched against the grey winter sky, and, although no bell had rung there for generations, a haunting eeriness clung to its walls. The scent of damp stone and the earthy smell of hidden moss crept from beneath the icy blanket.

Untouched snow lay thick across the ground, pristine apart from the delicate prints - tiny bird tracks clustered near the headstones and a single winding trail that might have been a fox passing through, seeking warmth and shelter. Ancient gravestones, some leaning and cracked, poked through the snow like forgotten sentinels.

A shiver ran down Mary's spine as they moved further into the burial ground, feeling as if they were trespassing in a place where only the past had permission to enter. 'Look, over there,' she said, pointing past the bell tower to the ivy covered headstone.

Rounding their way towards it, they froze. There, slumped against the rough, weathered stone, sat the body of Elwin Crawford, his face as pale as the frost glistening around him. His lifeless eyes stared blankly into the distance, frozen open in a hollow gaze. He'd been carefully propped up, his back against the stone, as though someone had placed him there purposefully. His hands rested limply in his lap, but between his fingers, he clutched a sign – its blood-red letters jagged and uneven, as though painted in a frenzy.

The sign read, '*Good Tidings of Terror. Who will be next - ho, ho, ho.*'

A baseball bat lay beside Elwin's staged figure, its handle splintered and worn. The wood was darkened near the barrel, as though from years of use, it carried a threatening aura. The faint trace of something dark marred its edge, chilling Mary's bones as her gaze shifted to the large bruise on the side of Elwin's head - a bloom of purple and black against the greyish-blue tinge of death.

The flashing blue light from the police cars cast harsh shadows across the old cemetery. Officers moved carefully through the grounds, murmuring as they examined the scene. Mary, Jenny, and Minister Brodie sat on a nearby bench, thick woollen blankets wrapped tightly around their shoulders. Despite the layers, each shivered - from the cold and the horror of what they'd found.

A young officer approached, holding a small notebook, his expression calm but concerned. He knelt to their level, his eyes briefly scanning their drawn faces before speaking. 'I know this is difficult, but if you could start from the beginning, it would help us. Who found the body first?'

Mary swallowed, her voice shaky. 'We found him together, he was slumped against the headstone.' She trailed off, clutching the edge of the blanket tightly.

Jenny reached for Mary's hand, giving it a gentle squeeze. She looked at the officer and added, 'We had been following clues - something cryptic that Elwin had left in his carol sheet. We thought . . . we never imagined it would lead us to . . .'

The officer nodded, jotting down a few notes, his expression softening as he listened. Another officer poured each of them a tea from a large flask, its steam rising in wisps through the cold air. Minister Brodie took a sip from the plastic cup, his usually composed face clouded with worry as he looked up at the officer. 'Elwin . . . he was one of us. Quiet, but with a kind soul,' he began, his voice cracking slightly. 'Whatever brought him to that grave wasn't just some whim.'

The young officer exchanged a glance with his colleague, then cleared his throat. 'We'll need to take your statements, all of you. And we'll have a team out here to check every inch of this cemetery.' His gaze drifted toward the bell tower, then back to the three of them. 'I'll have someone escort you all back to the Manse. You shouldn't be out here in the cold any longer.'

'Thank you,' Mary said. 'That would be so kind.'

The manse felt like a sanctuary, but the weight of tragedy hung heavily as Mary, Minister Brodie, and Jenny sat around the worn wooden table in the dining room. Each of them sipped a small sweet sherry, their hands trembling as they tried to process the horror of what they'd seen.

Jenny broke the silence first, her voice quiet as she murmured. 'We need to piece together what we know about Elwin. There are too many unanswered questions.' She looked at Mary, who nodded in agreement.

'All this talk about family secrets,' Mary said, disbelief creeping into her voice. 'Hilda is the only person who has mentioned Elwin had a brother, yet he never spoke of him to anyone. Why wouldn't he talk about Arthur? And if Arthur does exist, why did Elwin become the sole inheritor of their parents' estate?'

Minister Brodie leaned back in his chair, a troubled expression crossing his face. 'Elwin was always a private man. Maybe he wanted to distance himself from his past. But if Arthur was looking for him in Hollybrook, that raises a lot of questions. What was his intention? Did he want a reconciliation?'

Mary shook her head, her fingers nervously tracing the rim of her glass. 'And what about Elwin's behaviour in the weeks leading up to his death? It was as if he didn't recognise people. He even avoided me at church, and that was unusual for him. He loved the community, and the music - he was always at the forefront of the clapping. It's like he was a different person altogether.'

'That's right,' Jenny said, her eyes widening. 'Maggie Deans saw him at the train station but he reacted as if she were a total stranger.'

'Something must have been troubling him,' Minister Brodie murmured. 'And then there's the mysterious woman who he was dating. Who is she? Was she involved in any of this? Did she know about his family troubles?'

Mary set her glass down. 'Yes, we need to find out who she is. Maybe she can shed some light on what was going on. And what about the payday lenders? None of this sounds like Elwin.'

Jenny's eyes darted around the room as if searching for answers in the very walls. 'Lucy Hamilton said that a relative had turned up unannounced. What if it's Arthur, and he's here in Hollybrook, seeking revenge for Elwin inheriting his parents' estate?'

'And what if Elwin's death isn't just about him?' Minister Brodie asked. 'What if there are other players in this? Like you say, Mary. We have the mystery woman, Arthur, and the money lenders. What if it's all connected? There could be a larger web of deceit we haven't even begun to untangle.'

The three sat in heavy silence, the enormity of their realisations weighing on them. Outside, the wind howled softly against the windows, but within the manse, their resolve began to harden. They had to dig deeper, uncover the truth behind Elwin's life, and understand the demons that loomed over him in his final days.

. . .

The next day, Mary made her way back to the vestry, pushing open the heavy door. Her heart raced at the sight of Elwin's coat and scarf hanging dejectedly on his peg. She stepped closer, a lump forming in the back of her throat as she cautiously checked the pockets. Her fingers glided over the fabric, finally brushing against the smooth surface of his mobile phone and the crisp edge of a neatly folded letter. Taking a deep breath, she read the note before gathering the items. The contents of the note weighed heavier than the pull of the phone in her pocket, as she headed back to the Manse.

'Look what I found in Elwin's coat,' she said, placing the letter and phone on the table. 'I think we might be able to find something useful if we can access it.'

They tried code after code, fumbling through numbers that Elwin might have chosen - his house number, the year he'd joined the church, even the date of the annual Christmas service. Each attempt was met with the same stubborn refusal of the locked screen.

Minister Brodie rubbed his forehead, muttering, 'It must be something meaningful to him.'

Mary's eyes lit up with a sudden thought. 'What about his date of birth?'

Minister Brodie glanced up, eyebrows raised, then shuffled over to his drawer where he kept a record of parishioners' details. Pulling out the log, he thumbed through until he found Elwin's name and read out the date in numbers. Mary keyed it in. The screen unlocked, allowing them entry to Elwin's digital world. His last voice and text messages and a series of missed calls all waited.

'Let's see what he was up to,' Jenny said, her eyes gleaming with curiosity as she took the phone from Mary and began scrolling. She finally landed on a picture stored in Elwin's messages. 'Here, Look at this.' The photo showed a pretty lady with a bright smile, her face framed by soft, curly red hair, and sparkling green eyes.

According to the texts going back and forth, her name is Amanda,' Jenny said. 'I saw this lady last week in the Cozy Corner Café. Perhaps Elwin was too embarrassed to admit he had a lady friend staying over.'

'Let's see if we can find her social media profile,' Mary said. 'That should tell us more about her, as long as her settings are not private.'

As Amanda's profile loaded, a stream of photos flooded the screen. Smiling alongside Elwin in picture after picture, she looked every bit as if she were in a joyful relationship with him. Her posts brimmed with snapshots of them together, each one capturing intimate, happy moments. But as they scrolled through her timeline, a growing sense of confusion settled over them. The photos of Elwin appeared oddly placed, interspersed in a way that didn't make sense - moments seemingly out of order, creating a puzzling, disjointed timeline.

'Wait a minute,' Mary said, realising something was off. 'None of this adds up. These pictures hint at a relationship that's lasted for years.'

Mary pulled out her own mobile, searching through her contacts until she found Hilda's number. With a quick tap, she dialled. After a few seconds, Hilda's familiar voice came through. Mary switched to loudspeaker, glancing at her friends, 'Hilda, you're on speaker with me, Jenny and Minister Brodie.'

'Is everything alright?' Hilda asked. 'Rumours are flying around that Elwin's dead and we have a Christmas serial killer on the rampage. Who would ever have imagined that - in Holly-brook of all places.'

'Hilda, I need to ask you something important about Elwin and his brother.' Mary paused, letting out a long breath. 'Was Arthur . . . was he Elwin's twin?'

There was a brief silence before Hilda replied. 'Yes, Mary,

Arthur was his identical twin. I swear, you would never be able to tell them apart.'

Mary hung up, exchanging a grave look with Jenny and Minister Brodie. 'We need to know,' she said, her words coming slowly as if she was still in the process of piecing all parts of the puzzle together. 'How long Elwin has been dead? And how long Arthur has been . . . playing the part of his brother.'

Jenny swallowed, the gravity of Mary's words settling over her. 'Do you think he's been pretending for weeks? Months, even?'

Mary pressed her fingers to her lips. 'I think he only pretended when he needed to, even when Elwin was alive. But I believe Christmas Eve, for whatever reason, was the night he tried to fool the whole of Hollybrook. Perhaps he thought he was going to be found out, and that's when he sneaked out of the church.'

Minister Brodie's face grew serious. 'If Arthur was able to fool us all, he must've planned this deception meticulously.' He rubbed his chin thoughtfully. 'The autopsy report might be the only way to untangle the full extent of his deception.'

When Mary, Jenny, and Minister Brodie entered the police station, a quiet hush filled the sterile lobby, broken only by the faint hum of fluorescent lights overhead. The place seemed almost too calm for a supposed serial killer being on the loose.

As they approached the front desk, Mary felt her heart pounding, each beat echoing the urgency of their findings. She glanced at Jenny and the minister, both looked equally tense. 'We need to speak with Officer Harper,' Mary said. 'I called ahead and briefed him, so he's expecting us.'

The receptionist acknowledged their presence and gestured for them to follow her down a narrow corridor to a small meeting room. They entered, finding Officer Harper seated at the table, a hint of curiosity in his smile. 'You've certainly been a busy trio,' he remarked, motioning for them to take a seat. 'Now, what is it you have for me?'

Mary placed Elwin's phone and the folded note on the table. 'We've uncovered some disturbing information about Elwin's brother, Arthur, and a woman named Amanda,' she began. 'The note here.' She tapped it with her fingers. 'Which I found in Elwin's pocket, helps fill in some of the gaps.'

Jenny shifted in her seat. 'We believe they were trying to scam Elwin out of his savings. When he caught on to their scheme . . .' She let the implication linger, her eyes darting between Mary and Officer Harper.

'Exactly,' Minister Brodie interrupted. 'It seems they murdered him to keep him quiet. But it doesn't stop there. They devised a plan to create the notion of a serial killer being on the loose to divert attention from their crime.'

Mary nodded, continuing the thread. 'It was they who staged Elwin's body near the old bell tower, hoping it would throw everyone off their scent. Then Arthur went to the Christmas Eve Service pretending to be Elwin. This would give them more time to do whatever they were doing.'

'And Amanda,' Jenny added, 'She was most probably the person lurking in the graveyard, wielding a baseball bat. She was waiting for someone to see her, to create the illusion of the serial killer roaming the church grounds.'

'We started following what we believed were clues written on the margins of Elwin's music sheets.' Mary explained. 'Though they may appear disconnected from the unfolding events, they certainly led us to Elwin's body. I suspect some of them pertain to a cold case - a person who has been missing for a long time. Elwin knew her before moving to Hollybrook.' She nodded toward the note. 'And there's certainly more to uncover.'

Officer Harper listened intently, his expression shifting from curiosity to concern as he reached for the note. Unfolding it, he read it aloud.

'To whoever finds this' . . . he started, pausing briefly to gather his thoughts before continuing. *'If you are reading this, then my suspicions were not the ramblings of a man thinking he was on the verge of madness, but of a man who was in danger and is now dead. After Lydia, I never thought I could ever fall in love again. Her disappearance and not knowing what happened to her still haunts my dreams. However, I met a woman, a beautiful lady called Amanda, who I thought would enable me to have a second chance at love, and happiness. It was all going well until I found she was already in a relationship with my brother, Arthur, and that the two of them were plotting to drive me mad and steal all my savings. I'm sure they have been poisoning me, a little bit at a time, as I often feel unwell and forgetful. Rather than confront them, I will investigate the extent of their treachery, as I now believe Arthur had a hand in Lydia's disappearance too. Should it all go wrong, then take this along with my phone to the police. I have emails from my lawyer and the bank that pertain to matters I did not instruct. Arthur does not know yet, but I have already contacted the fraud department and they are looking into the signature. Should anything happen to me before then, please inform the police and make sure Lydia is found and laid to rest.*
  Yours sincerely
  Elwin Crawford

Officer Harper rose from his seat, the note from Elwin still clutched in his hand. 'I'll have a team investigate all of this immediately. We'll gather more evidence and launch a thorough search for Arthur and Amanda. It all seems a bit fragmented at the moment, but we'll investigate every angle.'

As they stepped out of the station, a wave of relief washed over Mary. They had untangled the threads of a sinister plot, but the tragic end of Elwin pressed heavily on her heart. 'We did our best,' she said, her voice laced with sorrow. 'I'm sorry Elwin couldn't tell us what was happening. Perhaps if he had, he'd still be alive.'

'Indeed,' Minister Brodie replied, placing a reassuring hand on Mary's shoulder. 'Now it's time to honour Elwin's memory and ensure that justice prevails.'

'But there's still the mystery surrounding Lydia,' Jenny said, her heart sinking. 'I don't think Elwin will be able to rest in peace until that mystery is solved.'

'I'm sure it will only be a matter of time,' Minister Brodie, said with a knowing smile.

Jenny and Minister Brodie sat at the dining table, where Mary's magnificent homemade steak pie took centre stage, the steam rising invitingly. Fluffy mashed potatoes, golden-brown roasties, and creamy cauliflower in cheese sauce completed the feast. Just as they were about to dig in, a loud knock came from the front door.

Mary exchanged a puzzled glance with her friends before rising. 'The only visitors I ever receive on New Year's Day are you two. I wonder who else it could be?'

Standing on the doorstep was Officer Harper, a huge smile covering his face. 'I have good news,' he said, stepping inside, the chill of the outside air trailing behind him.

Mary invited him in. 'We were just about to eat. I can set an extra place as we have plenty to go around.'

'No, thank you. I'm on my way home and Betty will have a feast waiting.' He did, however, take a seat at the table. 'We found Arthur and Amanda. They're in custody now.'

Mary's heart raced, the pie momentarily forgotten. 'What happened?' she asked, feeling a whirlwind of emotions.

'Arthur was apprehended after we pieced together the time-line. Elwin's death occurred just before Christmas Eve. We found poison in his system, but the blow to the head was what ultimately killed him. It seems Arthur discovered that Elwin was snooping into their plans and decided to take drastic action. The payday lenders were Arthur's means of finance until he had full access to Elwin's funds.'

Minister Brodie's expression hardened, his hands clenching the edge of the table. 'And what about Lydia?'

'Arthur confessed to her murder as well,' Officer Harper continued. 'He had become jealous of her affections toward Elwin. Thinking he could win her love, he lured her on a date pretending to be his brother. When she realised it was Arthur, she threatened to expose him to the village. In their argument, he pushed her, and she fell. He claims it was never his intention to kill her. So, in his panic, hid the body rather than report it.'

Mary felt a mix of relief and sorrow. 'I'm glad he's cooperating.'

'Yes,' Officer Harper replied, leaning forward. 'And he's doing so fully, and will take us to where Lydia's body is hidden so she can finally be laid to rest.'

A silence fell among them, as they contemplated this news. 'Thank you,' Mary said, feeling relieved it all seemed to be over. 'It was kind of you to stop by and let us know.'

Officer Harper nodded, gratitude in his eyes. 'This would never have been solved without the three of you and your sleuthing. Your efforts made all the difference.'

With glasses raised high, the three friends clinked their crystal flutes together, in a bittersweet toast to Elwin's cherished memory, the long-awaited peace of finding Lydia, and the hope of a brighter, happier New Year ahead.

BIO:

Having had a passion for reading and writing since an early age, this passion has only grown over the years. Marti M. McNair has been writing since she could pick up a pen and after her children flew the nest she turned to writing seriously. Her main focus is writing for a YA audience, and her books feature dystopian settings, dark political undercurrents and places her characters in precarious situations which tests them to the limit. She was the winner of the prestigious Scottish Association of Writers, Barbara Hammond Prize. She is also a partner in Auscot Publishing and retreats and a graphic designer for Writers' narrative eMagazine.

https://www.martimcnair.com

Chapter Three

DECK THE HALLS WITH MISTLETOE AND MURDER

by Sheena Macleod

It is two weeks before Christmas, and a wedding is causing mayhem in the village of Lochside in the Scottish Highlands. With so many villagers invited, everyone is running late. The hairdresser is behind schedule, the caterers are stuck in drifting snow, and the band has turned up early. With so much going on, no one notices that the groom has gone missing.

When a member of the wedding party is found dead with a sprig of mistletoe covering their mouth, Fiona McGregor, landlady of the Loch Tarry Inn, turns sleuth to investigate. She uncovers secrets from the past that someone wants kept hidden. Has the missing groom murdered a member of the wedding party, or is someone else to blame? Can Fiona find the groom and identify the killer before any more of the wedding party go missing or are murdered?

A Christmas Scottish Cozy Mystery

As Fiona McGregor waited to cross the street, a large, dark green sports car, the likes of which she'd never seen before, flashed past, horn hooting and sending sprays of slush sideways.

'Urgh! What in all honesty was that?' she asked Alistair MacIntosh, the piper, who appeared on the snow-covered pavement beside her.

Alistair grinned and clutched his bagpipes closer to his chest with one hand, while holding down his kilt with the other. 'That's some car, isn't it?' he said, tracking the large, dark green vehicle's trajectory as it made its way through the village. 'It would have cost a few bob too. I wouldn't mind a shot in that mean machine.'

'Mean Machine! More like a Green Monster. Likely it will be one of John Reilly's posh wedding guests,' she said as she wiped slush off the front of her jeans.

Alistair's grin grew wider, making freckles dance across his face. His ginger hair had been freshly trimmed, and he was dressed in the full Scottish traditional outfit, complete with jacket and sporran, and a *sgian-dubh* tucked into the side of one of his knee-length socks. 'That's the groom, Jamie Gold,' he said. 'I'm tae stand outside and pipe everyone intae the church. Jamie had been giving me my instructions. And, wow! Look.' He pointed to a huge psychedelic painted van sitting outside the Loch Tarry Inn. 'The band are here. They are ace. I can't wait tae hear them play. Mind you, they could have done so much better. Set for big things, they were.'

Fiona rolled her eyes and pulled the hood of her red parka up against the chilling wind. The snow had started again. And, more to the point, she didn't have time to stand here idly chitchatting about *Rockin Robin*. She had a wedding to prepare for, and attend. Unable to wait any longer for her turn in the hairdresser's over-filled schedule, she'd removed herself from the queue at *Perfect Cut's Salon* and was now making her way home to the Loch Tarry Inn to finish setting up for the reception. At this rate, she would never get everything ready in time.

'Right, Alistair. It's blowing a hoolie. Hold on to your kilt and follow me. I've gone twenty-seven years without knowing what a Scotsman wears under there, and I've no intention of finding out now,' she said and set off across the road at a brisk pace.

Alistair was still trotting behind Fiona when she entered the hotel foyer. The welcoming wreaths of holly and ivy and the decorated Christmas tree created a warm, festive feel. Satisfied, Fiona made her way into the lounge to speak to her mother, while Alistair headed off to find the band.

With only two weeks to go until Christmas, Fiona's friend Jo Reilly was getting married. The ceremony would start at two o'clock in the church, followed by a meal at the Loch Tarry Inn and then on to the village hall, where the wedding guests could dance and make merry late into the evening. It was a traditional Scottish wedding, complete with tartan kilts, sporrans, and pipers. And resident sleuth, more by accident than design, and landlady of the Loch Tarry Inn, Fiona McGregor, was running late. To be fair, so were most of the wedding guests.

As the bride was a local lass, and her father a wealthy farmer and big shot chair of the Church Committee, almost everyone in the village had been invited. And therein lay the problem. The hairdresser, who had squashed in every pleading request for an appointment, had fallen behind schedule, the caterers hadn't arrived yet, and the band, *Rockin Robin*, had arrived early with their roadie and were milling around in the function room, which Fiona needed to get ready for the caterers to set up in, when they did finally arrive. And to top it all, a strong wind was swirling snow from the fields into deep drifts around the village. Some of the locals seemed to be on top of it all and were doing a grand job of keeping the main walkways free of snow. But it didn't look like the weather would be settling any time soon.

As Fiona settled herself onto one of the tall stools in front of the bar, her mum, Carol, slid a warming cup of coffee across the counter towards her and said, 'Here's hoping no one else needs a bed for the night. Ha! There's no more room at the Inn.'

Fiona smiled and felt herself relaxing. 'Aw Mum. That's the least of our worries. The caterers were meant to be here over an hour ago, and there's still no sign of them. And, anyone who needs a bed for the night can bunk up in the village hall. We've enough bedding to go around... even if all of Santa's elves and the three wise men turn up here too.'

Carol guffawed. 'But really, I'm not surprised about the caterers. Reports have been coming in all morning on the radio of drifting snow blocking the main roads. Looking on the bright side, though, snow ploughs are out trying to clear a passage into and out of the village.' She picked up a bottle of cleaning spray and started wiping down the bar.

As Fiona sipped her coffee, her thoughts turned to the wedding. Her once 'bestest', best friend, Joanne Reilly, Jo to everyone who knew her, was getting married. Jo had left the village four years earlier to train as a veterinary nurse and had now returned with a husband-to-be in tow.

'By all accounts, Mum, the groom is a bit of a big shot in horse breeding and training.'

Carol paused, the cleaning cloth still clutched in her hand. 'Oh! That will suit John Reilly. The 'Laird of Lochside' will be pleased about that.'

Fiona nodded her agreement. As far as Fiona and most of the other villagers were concerned, Jo's father was an out-and-out snob. And arrogant with it. When anyone of importance was nearby, John Reilly spoke as if he had marbles in his mouth, but Fiona knew that his real accent sounded more like he was munching on gravel. Everyone called him 'The Laird of Lochside' behind his back, including his daughter Jo, who was nothing like her father. Jo was down to earth and so laid back she was almost horizontal.

But none of this stopped the excitement coursing through Fiona. Above everything else, she loved weddings, particularly a white, winter wedding. Not that she had ever been a bride herself. Hmm! One day perhaps. But that day wasn't yet. She had still to meet Mr Right. And, she was in no hurry. No, today was Jo's wedding day, and Fiona couldn't be more excited, she thought as she headed upstairs for a quick shower.

Fiona wound extra-large rollers into her long, dark hair. She laid out her wedding outfit, ready to change into later, before heading down to the lounge to restore some order. When her father had died three years earlier, Fiona inherited the Loch Tarry Inn from him. Her mother, Carol, who was willing to spend time behind the bar serving customers and gossiping with them, had never shown any interest in taking over the management of the eight-bedroomed hotel. This suited Fiona, who loved being the landlady of the Loch Tarry Inn.

By the time Fiona arrived in the lounge, Slade was belting out *Merry Xmas Everybody* on the jukebox, and the caterers were filing through the front door, which had been wedged open, letting in the chilling air. Thank goodness for the blazing fire in the lounge, she thought as she pulled the door closed behind them.

'Our van just missed being hit by a falling tree,' one of the caterers said to Fiona. 'We were lucky. It came down after we passed. I doubt anyone else will get through until it's removed.'

Fiona shook her head and wondered if the wedding would have to be cancelled. At least the caterers had arrived. And a fallen tree could be removed easily enough. Regardless, she would still have to set everything up and be ready on time. Letting out a deep sigh of frustration, she directed the catering team back outside and pointed to a door leading into the kitchen. When she was satisfied that the caterers knew where to unload, she shrugged on her parka and heralded the band, the roadie, and the piper outside, making sure to pull the front door firmly closed behind them.

'You lot. Follow me,' she called and marched them next door

to the village hall. She held on to the hood of her parka, to stop her rollers falling out, and scanned the church nestled in its own grounds at the back of the hall, but could see no sign of the minister's car outside. The church at Lochside shared a minister, and the manse was in one of the other villages. No doubt, the minister would be arriving soon. Or, he could already be here, clinking glasses and swilling malt whisky with the 'Laird of Lochside', she thought. She smiled at the nickname used for John Reilly. It had been Jo who'd started calling her father 'The Laird' and the name had stuck

As she marched towards the village hall, she thought about her once 'bestest' friend, who was now only a friend. Although they'd kept in touch, they'd grown apart since Jo moved away. The special bond that had formed between them as they'd grown up together had loosened. Fiona hadn't even met the new man in her friend's life, although she had heard all about Jamie Gold from Jo. And, by the looks of the flash car the groom was running around in, he was every bit as successful as Jo claimed. Well, as long as Jo is happy, she thought as she led the four members of the band plus the lone piper into the village hall, while their roadie drove their van around and reversed outside the back of the hall so he could unload their instruments. Which, by the size of the psychedelic painted van, held a mass of equipment.

The band members wore tartan kilts and black t-shirts. They were all friends of Jo. As the band made their way inside, they each introduced themselves to Fiona as they passed.

'Donnie, the drummer.'

'Lucy. I'm the bass guitarist.' She perched a hand on her hip, as if daring Fiona to say anything. 'Aye, I'm a lassie, but don't tell the lads.'

'Keith. Erm! Keyboards.'

"And I'm Steve Logan. Lead singer and guitarist.'

Fiona gasped as she stepped into the village hall behind them. It looked like a winter wonderland. Truly magical. The village hall committee had excelled themselves over their decorations from previous years. A large Christmas tree stretched up to the ceiling. Hundreds of white lights and dozens of sparkling white turtle doves glittered out a festive welcome. Fiona's tree in the foyer of the Loch Tarry Inn paled in comparison. Sprigs of fresh mistletoe hung above the doors and around the semicircular bar that had been set up in a corner of the hall. Small star-shaped lights on hanging strings stretched around the walls, and across the front of the stage, where Fiona instructed the band to set up. She left them to it and set off to sort out the caterers.

Dressed in a green, long-jacketed trouser suit, with her make up applied and her dark hair brushed out into long waves, Fiona finally felt ready to make her way to the church. She had given strict instructions to her mother, who wasn't attending the service, to keep the caters on track until she returned. She wanted no mishaps.

Hearing the drone of bagpipes starting up, Fiona pulled on her woollen, full-length functional, if well-worn, green coat. She slithered through the snow in her leather ankle boots, trying to make it over to the church without falling. Although it was still bitterly cold, Fiona joined the others milling about outside to listen to Alistair piping the arrival of the wedding guests. Word had circulated around the village that Jo would travel to the church in style. Fiona, along with the other guests, had arrived promptly to see the bride arriving. A few moments later, Alistair stopped playing. Church bells rang. When the bells stopped, Fiona leant forward to get a better view of an approaching white sleigh, pulled by a grey horse. Silver bells jingled out the bride's approach.

Fiona gasped as Jo stepped from the sleigh. A full-length white wedding dress peeked out between the folds of a long red velvet cape, trimmed around the hood with white fur. Jo had one hand inside a white fur muff and in her other hand she held a bouquet of purple thistles. Two bridesmaids stepped out behind Jo, wearing long-sleeved red dresses, trimmed with white fur around the hem and cuffs. A page boy appeared, wearing a tartan kilt and a thick Harris tweed jacket. He was followed by a young girl in a white dress and white fur cape. As the wedding party made their way up to the church, the girl threw red rose petals into the bride's path.

Fiona joined the other guests as they hurried into the church ahead of the bride, to await her entry. Both ushers greeted Fiona as she passed through the door. The groom and his best man were already in place at the front of the church. Fiona's eyes widened at the sight of the best man in his kilt. '*Phwoar!* she thought. She saw the resemblance between the best man and his brother, Jamie Gold. But, the warmth reflected in the best man's dark eyes and warm smile, told Fiona that she wouldn't find him behind the wheel of any monster of a car, unlike his brother. It was the first time, in a very long time, that Fiona had felt such an instant attraction to anyone. And, she now fully understood why Jo was marrying Jamie Gold.

No sooner had Fiona settled onto a pew when the father-of-the-bride strode to the front of the church and held up a clenched hand. The organ player stopped playing, and John Reilly stepped up to the pulpit, his face a deep shade of red.

'The minister has been delayed,' John Reilly said and wiped sweat from his brow with the back of his hand. 'Apparently, a tree is blocking the road and, with the drifting snow, there is no way the minister can get through until the tree and the drifts have been cleared. The minister will get here as soon as he can. So, although it is not the usual order for a wedding, please head over to the Loch Tarry Inn where hot and cold drinks plus sandwiches will be served to tide you over until the minister arrives. Let's not let this delay spoil this very special day for *my* daughter.

'As, by tradition, the bride and groom are not meant to see

each other before the wedding ceremony, the best man, the ushers and myself will leave through the back door and escort the groom over to the village hall where we will wait with him until the church service *can* take place.' He let out a forced guffaw. 'The caterers will be serving us with drinks and snacks there too. He beckoned with his hand to his future son-in-law, 'Jamie, lead the way.'

Fiona headed over to the village hall with them, to check on the catering arrangements there. It could take an hour, if not more, she reckoned, for the tree and drifts to be cleared and for the minister to get here.

When they arrived in the hall, the band had set up and were jamming together on their musical instruments. Fiona stood at the front of the stage and held up a hand. The drummer stopped drumming, and the others followed his lead.

After Fiona had explained to everyone who had been in the hall what was happening, the lead singer, Steve Logan, held out his guitar. He called to one of the two caterers who were setting up the bar. 'Come up and give us a song, Joel. Something Christmassy.'

A shaven-headed man in his mid-twenties threw off his white catering coat and jumped up on to the stage. After chatting with the band members for a few minutes while he strummed along with them, Joel turned around and belted out the first chords of Mariah Carey's hit song, *All I Want for Christmas is You*, on the guitar.

When Joel opened his mouth and sang, Fiona stopped in her tracks. She couldn't have walked out the hall if she had tried. Joel had the most mesmerising voice she'd ever heard, and it suited the band perfectly. They were made for each other. As she wandered over to the front of the stage, Fiona realised with a jolt who Joel was. With his shaven head and gaunt face, she hadn't recognised the long-haired youth she and Jo had grown up with. But, she did now. Joel had left Lochside around the same time that Jo had left to go to college.

After Joel finished playing the last chords of the song, he followed up by singing the duet *Peace on Earth/ Little Drummer Boy* with Steve Logan, accompanied by the band. As Fiona listened to the hit song, recorded and made popular by David Bowie and Bing Crosbie, all the stresses of the day disappeared.

Joel finished the number to great applause. He handed the guitar back to Steve Logan and leapt from the stage.

John Reilly paced in front of the bar waiting to order a round of drinks. He 'hmphed and hawed' loud enough to draw Fiona's attention, before he turned and pointed at Joel. 'Stop messing about and get on with what I'm paying you to do. Serving drinks to *me* and *my* guests.'

Joel scuttled back behind the bar and proceeded to take John Reilly's drinks order, his face a deep shade of scarlet.

Twenty minutes later, Fiona was surprised to hear the groom and his future father-in-law arguing through gritted teeth, as they made their way towards the back door of the village hall, drinks in hand. From what Fiona could make out, John Reilly wasn't happy with how the wedding was going so far, and the groom wasn't happy with his future father-in-law. She left them to it.

Fiona arrived back in the lounge of the Loch Tarry Inn to find empty Champagne bottles littering the counter of the bar, and the sound of the mother-of-the-bride wailing as she sat on a stool in front of them. 'I am married to an Ass,' Mrs Reilly said to Carol, who stood at the other side of the bar polishing glasses and nodding to the irate woman.

Carol raised her eyes at Fiona, as if to say *I've got this*. Fiona gathered up the empty bottles and placed them into the recycle bin.

Mrs Reilly swivelled around on her seat to face her daughter. 'Think twice before going through with this wedding, Jo. Don't make the same mistake I did when I married your father. Take the minister not turning up as an omen. Oh, if I knew then what I know now,' she said between sobs, 'I wouldn't have turned up either.'

Fiona wondered just how much Champagne Jo's mother had consumed. The bridesmaids, who were ignoring the weeping woman, were clustered around a table with the bride, sipping Champagne and laughing, as they competed to see who could come up with the best 'jilted by the vicar joke'.

'What do you call a vicar breaking the speed limit to get to a wedding? Jo asked. 'Rev,' she spluttered, and Fiona joined in with the laughter. It was a no brainer for Fiona between joining the bride and bridesmaids or consoling Jo's weeping mother, who now lurched forward.

'I'm going for a lie down in the bridal suite upstairs,' Jo's mother said as she slithered down from the stool. As she made her way out the lounge, she stopped in front of the three-tier wedding cake, decorated with tartan ribbon and purple thistles. 'Call me when this wedding finally gets started.'

Twenty minutes later the women around the table had polished off another bottle of Champagne, and Fiona couldn't finish telling her joke for laughing. She immediately sobered when the best man rushed in and announced, 'The minister has arrived.'

When Fiona and the others stood to leave, the best man held up his hands, palms out. 'But we can't find the groom and the father-of-the-bride. Erm! My brother, Jamie, and John Reilly appear to be missing. I think you'd all better sit down again.'

Fiona stood. There was no way she was staying put, and neither were the others by the look of them. She followed the bride and bridesmaids out the lounge and made her way with them over to the village hall.

As they neared the back of the hall, a loud scream, coming from behind the far side of the band's psychedelic painted van, pierced the relative silence. Arriving at the source of the sound, Fiona saw John Reilly lying on the ground, an empty whisky glass beside his clenched hand, his face turned upwards, his eyes vacant and staring sightless at the snow-filled sky.

Above him stood his wife, her hands over her mouth, her eyes bulging wide with surprise. One of the bridesmaids knelt beside John Reilly and felt his neck for a pulse. She shook her head. 'Nothing. Has someone phoned for an ambulance?'

Fiona tapped out the number for the emergency services and asked for an ambulance... and the police. Fiona bent forward to better see Jo's father. John Reilly lay on his back. Dressed in his wedding outfit of kilt, jacket and a plaid, Fiona could see no blood or any injuries on him. But over his mouth lay a sprig of mistletoe.

The best man ushered everyone away from the back of the hall. 'Come on, there's nothing that can be done here. One of the ushers has gone to fetch the doctor. Marion O'Hara will attend to things until the police get here.'

Fiona left with the others. As they gathered together in the lounge of the Loch Tarry Inn the chatter between everyone grew louder. Fiona stuck an index finger into each side of her mouth and gave a shrill whistle to gain their attention. 'Quiet,' she called. The police will be here as soon as they can. We have been instructed not to touch or disturb anything and to stay here until they arrive.'

Fiona circulated the room, trying to determine who had seen what. No one admitted to seeing anything. The first any of them knew something was amiss was when Jo's mum screamed.

The groom was still nowhere to be seen, and Fiona's concern grew for his safety. Where was Jamie Gold and had he killed his future father-in-law to be? It could have been a natural death but the sprig of mistletoe covering John Reilly's mouth said otherwise. The police and emergency services could take a while to arrive. The weather had taken a turn for the worse again, and by the accounts coming in over the radio, snow drifts were still blocking the roads into the village.

Fiona looked over at Jo, who was being comforted by her bridesmaids. What should have been the happiest day of her life was turning into a nightmare wedding. And the couple hadn't even been married yet. Some of the men had formed a search party and had set off to look for Jamie Gold. Everyone else waited in the warmth of the lounge for the police to arrive. Likely they would all need to give a statement, Fiona thought. Even the minister, who now sat beside the bride, rolling a glass of malt whisky between his hands.

The band and the two members of the catering staff who had been in the village hall arrived, looking pale faced and shaken. The band and their roadie sat down at one of the tables, and fell into conversation. The caterers joined the other catering staff in the kitchen, who were now making pots of stovies for the hungry guests to tide them over until the wedding meal could be eaten.

Determined to find out what had happened to John Reilly and find the missing groom, Fiona joined a table for two, where the piper sat on his own deep in thought. Alistair MacIntosh hadn't set off yet with the search party to look for the groom, and was as good a person as any to start her enquiries with. Fiona intended to speak to everyone and find out what she could. After all, the police could take long enough to get here.

Alistair chattered nine to the dozen to Fiona, as if he had to get the words out before he ran out of breath. 'I'd been listening to the band tuning up. Joel was awesome, wasn't he? He should have stayed with the band. I don't know what possessed him to leave when he did.'

'Stayed with them?,' Fiona repeated, unsure what Alistair was on about.

'Aye, Joel was lead singer and guitarist, before Steve Logan. When Joel left, the band were on their way to stardom. Don't get me wrong, *Rockin Robin* are good, but they're nothing like as good as the band they were then.'

'Okay, well,' Fiona muttered. 'That's all very interesting, but we need to find out what happened at the back of the village hall. When did you last see John Reilly and Jamie Gold?'

'In the village hall. No! It was when they were leaving the hall. Not long after Joel sang his pieces. They went out the back together. I never thought anything of it.'

'And you didn't see either of them again after that?'

'Uhm! No. I stayed in the hall until the best man announced that the minister had turned up. Everyone seemed to move at once to get ready to head back to the church. I was gathering up my bagpipes when the best man asked if anyone knew where his brother and John Reilly were. No one did. We did a quick scout around the hall, but there was no sign of either the groom or the father-of-the-bride. The ushers headed over to the church to see if they had already made their way there, while the best man headed off to let Jo know that the minister had arrived. Look, I best get going to join the search for Jamie.'

Fiona watched the piper leave. If what Alistair had said was correct, then he had no more information to give her. She made her way over to the band, who were clustered around a table deep in conversation.

Lucy looked up and nudged over to allow Fiona room to join them. Steve Logan pulled a chair over for her from another table. Fiona asked them the same questions she had asked the piper. The drummer had been the only one who had noticed the groom and Jo's father leaving the hall together.

'They were having a right old go at each other,' the drummer said. 'And no wonder. Nobody wants delays at a wedding. But it was just one of these things, really. We all just had to wait until the minister turned up.'

Fiona agreed. It seemed as if none of them had anything further to add. Well, not anything that would help her figure out what had happened to John Reilly and Jamie Gold. Joel was going around the tables offering coffee. The drummer waved him over.

'Joel,' Fiona said, and laid her hand on his arm to catch his attention. 'Could I have a quick word?' Joel flinched at her touch, and Fiona drew her hand back. 'I just wanted to ask if you'd seen or heard anything that could help us find Jamie.'

Joel frowned and dipped his head. He grunted a reluctant 'no' as he finished pouring out Fiona's coffee before moving away from the table.

Lucy shook her head and lowered her voice. 'Although he tried to make out differently, Joel took it badly when Jo split up with him. He was devastated. Soon after, he left the village and the band. It was as if he wanted nothing more to do with Lochside.'

'We were called *Five Gold Rings* back then,' the keyboard player added. 'Splitting up with Jo cost Joel, but it cost the band a heck of a lot more. We'd been booked to do our first big tour of Scotland. It never happened after Joel left.

'But we've got Steve Logan now,' Lucy said. 'The chance of fame we missed out on then will come again.'

'With, or without, Joel,' the drummer added.

Fiona hadn't really listened to the piper when he'd told her about Joel leaving the band and the impact it had on them all. She'd been living in Edinburgh at the time, and hadn't kept up with the events in the village then. Now, she realised that this had all happened because Jo had split up with Joel.' Fiona recalled now that Jo and Joel had been a couple at the time she'd left to go to university. Jo had even hinted at a possible engagement between them. Fiona needed to talk to Jo to find out more.'

❄

Fiona found Jo being consoled by her bridesmaids. Jo's mother had gone upstairs to the bridal suite along with the children and their mothers.

When Fiona slipped into a seat beside Jo, her friend turned to her with tear-filled eyes. 'Jamie's brother is the only member of his family that we invited to our wedding.'

'Had Jamie and his family fallen out?' Fiona asked.

Jo sniffed and dabbed her eyes with a tissue. 'Oh, no. Nothing like that. Jamie's parents died when the boys were in their early teens. Apart from his brother, Jamie has no other close family. He wanted his brother to be his best man today. That was all the family he needed.'

Fiona placed an arm around her friend. 'I promise Jo, I'll do everything I can to find out what happened to your father, and to find Jamie. The police shouldn't be much longer in getting here. Did you see Joel? He came with the caterers.'

'Not until he served me coffee a few moments ago. I was surprised to see Joel. I haven't seen him in years.'

'I heard he left the village not long after you did,' Fiona said.

'The split between us... Well, it just happened. We wanted different things. Jamie was on the brink of stardom with the band, and I was leaving to go to college. You'd already left by then to go to Uni, so you missed most of what happened around that time. After Joel and I split up... Well, I met Jamie. Dad approved,' Jo said and burst into a fresh flood of tears.

Fiona left Jo in the capable hands of the bridesmaids and joined her mother behind the bar.

'The police have been keeping me updated,' Carol said to her. 'They've spoken to Doctor O'Hara and have arranged for a police team to get here as soon as possible.' Carol lowered her voice. 'Marion O'Hara confirmed that John Reilly was dead when she got there.'

'Poor Jo. What a thing to happen, especially on her wedding day,' Fiona said. 'And then for her groom to go missing too.'

'Have you found out anything yet?'

After Fiona told her mother what she had seen and who she'd spoken to, Carol lowered her voice again, this time almost to a whisper. 'I keep mulling over what Jo's mother said as she sat at the bar earlier. "My husband's an Ass." And "If I'd known then what I know now, I wouldn't have married him." But, more importantly, why did she tell us that she was going to lie down upstairs and then head to the village hall? You need to talk to Jo's mother, Fiona. Mrs Reilly could be the last person to have seen her husband alive.'

Fiona nodded her agreement. 'What's been niggling me is why a sprig of mistletoe was placed on John Reilly's mouth? Why mistletoe? Do you think it could be significant?'

'A message perhaps... Of speaking of love or even of kisses,' Carol said.

Fiona shook her head, she couldn't make sense of it all. 'The mistletoe had to have been placed there by whoever killed John Reilly. Could the Laird of Lochside have been cheating on his wife? There is only one way to find out. I need to speak to Mrs Reilly.'

When Fiona entered the bridal suite, Jo's mum was nowhere to be seen. The children were clustered around the television watching a cartoon and eating bowls of stovies. They didn't raise their heads or seem to notice Fiona's presence in the room.

'I just wanted to check on Jo's mum,' Fiona said to one of the mothers.

The woman tilted her chin towards the open door of the bedroom.

Jo's mum lay on top of the bed, dabbing at her red and swollen eyes with the corner of a paper tissue The box lay by her side. Jo perched on the edge of the bed beside her.

'Are the police here yet?' Mrs Reilly asked. 'Likely they'll be blaming me. I swear, I never did anything to harm John. My husband had a dicky heart, you know. Ask Doctor O'Hara, she will tell you. John kept it quiet. Pride likely, that such a strong man as himself wasn't in perfect health.'

'John Reilly had a heart condition?' Fiona repeated. It was news to her and likely even Jo didn't know this. Was Mrs Reilly telling the truth? Had John Reilly died from a heart attack? But that didn't explain the sprig of mistletoe covering his mouth. Mrs Reilly was adamant she hadn't placed it there. So, who had?

'John was dead when I found him. I was going to go for a lie down, but decided to see if the minister had arrived. I went to the back of the village hall and walked around the side of the van, to check if the minister's car was parked outside the church. And there John was. Lying on the ground.' A fresh flood of tears turned into deep wracking sobs.

Once Mrs Reilly had composed herself, Fiona ask her about what she'd said earlier, when she'd been sitting at the bar. 'Amongst other things, you called him an Ass. What was that about?'

'John is... was... an Ass. Always wanting to impress everybody. Nothing but the best for him... and for Jo.'

Fiona tried to make sense of Mrs Reilly's words. What was she trying to tell her? 'What do you mean? Surely that's a good thing to want the best for Jo.'

Mrs Reilly let out a mirthless laugh. 'Except it was what *he* thought was best for Jo, not what Jo thought was best. It was always about what John wanted. Including his choice of husband for her. Believe me, Jo's marriage to Jamie Gold wouldn't have lasted five minutes with John Reilly around. She'd had other relationships, before Jamie. But her father always frightened the young men off. None of them came up to muster in John's eyes.'

'Like Joel,' Fiona said.

Mrs Reilly's mouth opened in surprise. She tilted her head towards Fiona. 'Aye. Exactly like Joel. All of them hounded away. But Joel lasted the longest. He seemed well able to resist her father's scare tactics. Until he no longer could.'

'What do you mean? I wasn't aware of this and I was Jo's best friend. Granted, I'd left for university by then. But still, I didn't know about any of this.'

'Jo's father was always putting Joel down, but not in the hearing of anyone who would stand up for him. About him singing in a band. Being a waster without a job. John even mocked Joel to his face, about the pretty girls he would meet up with when touring with the band.'

'Does Jo know about this?'

'Of course not. But her father repeatedly told Jo that Joel was a drug addict in the making, a hippie, a wastrel, and that playing in a band wouldn't put food on the table. He said that if she married Joel, she needn't come running to him when she was broke and had been abandoned by Joel for one of his groupie girlfriends. John tried to poison Jo's mind against him.'

'But Joel wasn't like that. Not that I can remember.'

'No. Joel was a lovely lad. He was besotted with Jo. But her father chipped away until Jo started to doubt Joel. I watched it happening. And, Jo didn't want to hold Joel back. She knew he was on the brink of stardom. But once he was on the road touring, Jo agreed with her father, she would rarely see him.'

'And did Joel know all this?'

'Of course, he did. And he wasn't happy about it.'

'What about Jamie Gold? Jo seemed to think her father approved of the match.'

Mrs Reilly snorted. 'Approve? He set Jamie up with Jo. The type of son-in-law *he* wanted.'

'Do you know where Jamie is now?'

'Of course not. I haven't seen him since...' Mrs Reilly's hand shot to her mouth. 'You don't think Jamie harmed my husband, do you?'

Fiona didn't know. The more she heard about John Reilly, the more her suspicions grew that he'd been murdered. Mrs Reilly remained adamant that she hadn't placed the sprig of mistletoe over her husband's mouth. If she hadn't, then someone else had. But who?

With a sudden thought, Fiona excused herself and made her way to the side of the village hall. They had been told to stay away from there, but she only needed a quick look inside to find the answer to something that puzzled her.

Taking care to remain quiet, Fiona crunched through packed snow as she made her way along the outer side wall of the village hall. Fortunately, the window she was heading towards was situated away from the back door, where the body of John Reilly lay. Stretching up on to the tip of her boots, she looked through the window. The lights were still on inside the hall.

She cupped both hands around her eyes and peered through the window. The mistletoe above the door leading through to the back of the hall was still in place. She scanned the room but couldn't see the front door, so had no idea if the sprigs of mistletoe were still hanging there. She had a clear view of the bar. But, no matter how much she scrunched her eyes, she could only see one of the five sprigs of mistletoe she'd seen there earlier.

Fiona's suspicion that the mistletoe covering John Reilly's mouth had come from the village hall, seemed to have been confirmed. And, if one of the missing sprigs had been placed over John Reilly's mouth, where were the other three? She needed to get inside the hall to find out.

A commotion arose outside the back door of the hall, providing Fiona with the opportunity she was looking for. The best man bellowed at the roadie to open the back door of the van so it could be searched. From the loud shouts between the roadie and the best man, Fiona made out that Jamie Gold had been found, alive and well inside. Fiona used the momentary distraction to slip in to the hall. She pulled a pair of leather gloves from her pocket and made straight for the bar.

Taking care not to disturb anything, she checked behind the bar. She picked up a long-handled metal spoon, used for mixing cocktails, and poked inside the open bin. Just as she had expected, she saw three abandoned green sprigs of mistletoe, but minus their white berries.

Taking care not to be seen, Fiona slipped out the front door of the village hall. She desperately wanted to find out what had happened to Jamie, but it would have to wait. She had other business to attend to. And from what she had already heard, Doctor O'Hara had been called for, and the best man and the roadie were helping Jamie over to a bed in the Loch Tarry Inn. She would speak to both Jamie and Dr O'Hara later, but first, she wanted to speak to the other member of the catering staff who had been serving behind the bar in the village hall.

She found the flustered woman in the kitchen, desperately instructing her small team of staff to transfer the roast duck, partridge, goose and all the traditional Christmas vegetables and trimmings into covered hotplates. When she saw Fiona, the woman placed her hands on her hips. 'What do you want me to do with this lot? I can keep it hot, but it's going to be wasted if it's not eaten within the next few hours.'

The woman looked near to tears, and Fiona felt for her. She stuck out a hand, 'Fiona McGregor, landlady of the Loch Tarry Inn.'

The woman who looked to be in her mid-forties, wiped her hand on a cloth before shaking Fiona's hand. 'Laura Carpenter, co-owner of *Just Go, Catering Service*. I own the business with my husband, Stan, she said and pointed to a red-faced man, mashing potatoes. 'Seriously, do you have any idea when people are likely to eat?'

'Everyone *will* need to eat at some point, I can't be more specific than that. No doubt they'll all be so hungry by the time the police have taken their statements that they will enjoy the food regardless of how long it's been kept hot. Can I have five minutes of your time? In private.'

Laura followed Fiona through to the snug bar, which had been kept clear for the police interviews. Once they were seated in front of the open fire, Fiona asked Laura if she'd seen anyone removing the mistletoe from above the bar.

'It's funny you should ask that,' she said and pulled off her net cap, revealing a head of short-cropped, bright red hair.

Fiona loved the look, but needed to keep Laura on track. 'You saw something?'

'Something and nothing, perhaps. But I thought it strange at the time. I was setting up the bar with Joel, when he said we needed more wine glasses. He was adamant there wouldn't be enough, and that it was best to ask for them now, rather than waiting until everyone arrived.'

Fiona, couldn't keep up. 'What's that got to do with the missing mistletoe?'

'I'm getting to that. The thing is, as I was heading out the hall to fetch the wine glasses, I looked back and saw Joel removing a sprig of mistletoe from above the bar.'

'And, why did he do that?'

'I've no idea. But when I returned with the glasses, I challenged him about removing the mistletoe. He said the sprigs were hanging loose and he didn't want the berries falling into people's drinks.'

'Hmm! How strange. They looked okay earlier. Did you see where Joel put them?'

'Uhm, no. I never thought to look. Why? Is it important?'

'It could be,' Fiona said, thinking about the mistletoe placed over John Reilly's mouth.

'After Jamie Gold and John Reilly went out the back together, did either yourself or Joel leave the hall?'

'Not that I can think of. We stayed there until we were asked to leave. After the body... After the father-of-the-bride was found. I heard he'd had a heart attack. Is that right? Has the groom been found yet? I heard them taking someone upstairs.'

'It would seem so, although I haven't seen Jamie yet,' Fiona said. 'I'd best let you get on.'

Fiona leant against the far corner of the lounge bar and signalled to her mother that she wanted to talk to her. Carol poured Chardonnay into a large wine glass and brought it over to Fiona. 'Right now,' Carol said, 'if you told me Santa had just landed on the roof of the Loch Tarry Inn in his sleigh, I'd believe you. This day couldn't get any stranger.'

Fiona took a gulp of the chilled wine and laid the glass down with a satisfied sigh. 'Actually, I was going to tell you that Rudolph wasn't with him this year. Talking of missing persons, rather than reindeer, what happened to Jamie Gold? Why do you think he was hiding in the back of *Rockin Robin's* van?'

'Hmm!' Carol uttered. 'He sure didn't go in there looking for Christmas crackers. From what the roadie told me, Jamie and John Reilly both felt sick and groggy. Jamie thought he was going to pass out. Realising that he couldn't make it back into the village hall, he opened the unlocked door of the van and dragged himself inside and up onto a mattress. He called to John Reilly to climb in too, but John never answered. The last thing Jamie recalled before passing out was pulling the door closed and tugging a blanket over himself. Jo, Jamie's brother and Doctor O'Hara are upstairs with Jamie now. Oh, and the police must have hitched a lift on the back of Santa's sleigh. They'll be here any minute.'

'Thanks, Mum. Look, I need to have a quick word with Doctor O'Hara and Jamie before the police get here. Gather everyone together in the lounge. Leave the kids and their mums upstairs, but get everyone else in here. Including the band and the caterers. I'll be back in a couple of minutes, hopefully with some answers about what happened to John Reilly and Jamie Gold.'

Five minutes later, as four police officers entered the lounge, Fiona returned with Jo, Doctor O'Hara, Jamie Gold and his brother. Jamie looked a bit worse for wear, but seemed otherwise okay. Jo gripped onto his arm as if she would never let him out of her sight again.

Sergeant Swan coughed to gain the attention of the large and growing crowd. 'Can someone tell me where Mr Reilly's body is? The area needs to be sealed off and the Scene of Crime Officers given access. We'll need to take statements from everyone, so stay where you are until an officer calls you. Can we have a room with some privacy?'

Doctor O'Hara stepped forward. 'Of course, Sergeant Swan. John Reilly was found at the back of the village hall. The minister can take your team there. But I think you should listen to what the landlady of the Loch Tarry Inn has to say first. I think Fiona McGregor will be able to provide answers to all of the questions you may have, including what happened to Mr Reilly.'

Sergeant Swan glared at Fiona. 'Not you again. Like the Ghost of Christmas Past, you keep intruding into my investigations. Okay, what have you got to say for yourself this time? And keep it brief.'

Fiona clapped her hands to gain everyone's attention. 'Many of you have spent the last few hours searching for Jamie Gold, while others have been searching for answers to what happened to John Reilly. Thankfully, I can say that both searches have been fruitful, and answers have been found. It's been a long and fraught day for all of us, but more so for the wedding party. So, I won't keep you any longer than needed.

'The tragic events of today are tied firmly to the past, in more ways than one. At the time of John Reilly's death, I was in the lounge with the wedding guests, except for the men from the wedding party who were in the village hall along with the band, their roadie and two members of catering staff. The only person to leave the lounge and go to the village hall during that critical time was you, Mrs Reilly. You'd fallen out with your husband earlier and remained bitter about it all morning. And, you were possibly the last person to see John Reilly alive.'

Mrs Reilly made to speak, but Fiona held up a hand to silence her. 'But, you were not the last person to see him alive. Jamie Gold was.'

'What?' Jamie Gold roared and placed his arm around Jo, who sobbed beside him. 'Pah! What a load of old nonsense. Let the police get on with their job of finding out who murdered John Reilly, because it most certainly wasn't me.'

As Sergeant Swan made towards Jamie, Fiona continued. 'I said that you were the last person to see John Reilly alive, and likely you were, Jamie. He died soon after you climbed into the warmth of the van. And luckily, you did, or the police would have been investigating two deaths today. As you lay unconscious, you could easily have died from hypothermia. John Reilly wasn't so fortunate.'

'My husband died from hypothermia,' Mrs Reilly said.

'No!' Fiona said. 'He suffered a heart attack.'

A collective chatter erupted around the room. Sergeant Swan held up a hand and roared, 'Quiet.'

'A heart attack triggered by being poisoned,' Fiona added, and her words restored the calm called for as everyone, including the police officers, looked at her in stunned silence. 'The mistletoe laid over John Reilly's lips was significant as to the motive for murdering him, but it was also the main clue as to how he was killed. We could easily have mistaken this for a natural death, but the sprig of mistletoe covering John Reilly's mouth told me otherwise. Why had it been placed there? And by whom?

'Today, I listened to one of the most beautiful singing voices I've ever heard. But behind that voice lies a tragic story of love, loss, and a need for revenge. Joel, you poisoned both John Reilly and Jamie Gold in an act of revenge for losing Jo because of John Reilly's lies about you. It also cost you your place in the band and the chance of stardom.

'You were seen taking down the sprigs of mistletoe from above the bar in the village hall. You removed and crushed the white mistletoe berries and added the juice into John Reilly and Jamie Gold's glasses before you served them.'

Doctor O'Hara stepped forward. 'John Reilly had a heart condition. I am as certain as I can be at this stage that he suffered a fatal heart attack as a result of ingesting extract of mistletoe berries.' She turned to Sergeant Swan. 'You will find a whisky glass beside one of John Reilly's hands, it hasn't been touched, and another in the van where Jamie Gold dropped it. You should have them both tested for the presence of white mistletoe berries.'

Joel turned to leave but was stopped by two policemen.

'Is this true?' Sergeant Swan asked Joel. 'Joel tried to wriggle free before resigning himself to his fate. He crumpled against one of the police officers. 'I never meant to kill John Reilly. The berries were only meant to make him sick, the same as they did to Jamie Gold. How was I to know John Reilly had a heart condition? I only wanted to destroy his special day, the same as he did to me. I didn't mean to destroy his life, too. Although he destroyed mine.'

'That's all very well to say that now, Joel,' Fiona said. 'But you knew that you had killed him. When you slipped out of the hall and placed the mistletoe over John Reilly's mouth, you knew then that he was dead. You had to leave a message, though, didn't you? Otherwise, his death wouldn't have been so meaningful.'

As two policemen escorted Joel out of the lounge, towards a waiting police car, he called back over his shoulder. 'Aye, I've been bitter for years about losing my place in the band and the chance of fame. I held more than a grudge towards *that* man, and with good reason. It should have been me marrying Jo today, not Jamie Gold.'

After everyone, including the band and the caterers, had eaten their fill, the minister, who was sitting at the top table with the main wedding party, rapped a knife against a glass.

'Can I have your attention?' the minister said. 'Please raise *your* glasses to the bride and groom. To Mr and Mrs Gold.'

Carol nudged Fiona in the side with her elbow and whispered, 'Has the vicar been on the whisky again?'

The piper leaned his hands on the table. He stood and thrust his head forward in the direction of the minister. 'Erm! Ah! Sorry, minister, but... Well, you see... '

Fiona watched the freckles bounce across Alistair MacIntosh's face as he struggled to find the words to tell the minister that no wedding ceremony had taken place. Aye, they'd all turned up to the church, and he had piped the guests in, and the bride had arrived on a white sleigh. They'd even eaten the wedding meal. But as for a wedding ceremony. Well, no! That part never happened.

'Thanks, Alistair, I'll take over from here,' Jamie Gold said. 'I would like to thank the minister for staying with Jo today. I would also like to inform you all that while you were setting up for this wonderful wedding feast, Jo and I were in the church with the minister. We said a prayer for Jo's father. Then we said our marriage vows in the presence of my brother and Jo's mother.

'So, on behalf of my wife and I. Ahem! I'd like to thank everyone for all their help today. We want you now to join in with celebrations that, although not as we had planned, we both now wish to go ahead.'

Carol clapped along with the others and then stood. 'Erm! Can I have your attention? Anyone who doesn't have a bed for the night, there's plenty of straw in the stables up at Lochside Farm. Or, you can kip in the village hall, where bedding and a full breakfast will be provided.'

As the applause died away, everyone seemed to move at once. Tables were cleared and pushed to the side. Carol headed back to the bar. The roadie turned up the volume on the jukebox and made some selections.

While the notes of *White Christmas* filled the lounge, snow fell outside. The bride and groom took to the floor for the first dance, and were soon followed by the bridesmaids and ushers.

As Fiona repositioned a chair, she turned and bashed the leg of it against the best man. 'Oops, sorry.'

He held out a hand to her. 'Charlie Gold.'

Phwoar, Fiona thought. Jamie Gold's brother was even nicer up close. She set the chair down and took Charlie's outstretched hand. 'Fiona McGregor, reluctant sleuth, and landlady of the Loch Tarry Inn. Would you like to dance?'

BIO:

Sheena Macleod is a published historical fiction author and a prize-winning and published short story writer. She lives in a seaside town on the East Coast of Scotland. You can find her online at https://www.sheenas-books.co.uk

Chapter Four

A FROSTY FIASCO

Marti M. McNair

In the quaint town of Jinglebell, where the winter sun-dappled streets seemed to whisper secrets to the gentle breeze, Jinglebell Sleuths, occupied a cosy, dimly lit office above the bustling main street. This private detective company was a haven of mystery and intrigue amidst the town's serene charm. It was an idyllic place of work, with a sense of time passing languidly, like honey dripping from a spoon.

Alice Frost, the lead detective with penetrating brown eyes, sat at her cluttered desk, engrossed in a word search puzzle. Her plump lips pursed in concentration as she scanned the grid for elusive words. With a victorious grin lighting her chubby face, she thrust her fist into the air. 'Found one.'

Opposite her, Marcus Green, her seasoned partner, lounged in his worn office chair. With a furrowed brow, he scratched his balding head, engrossed in instructions on how to build a garden shed.

'Murder,' Alice said, a shiver running through her body.

Marcus's eyes widened. 'There's been a murder . . . here in Jinglebell? Four weeks before Christmas?' he said, suddenly alert of a potential case.

'No, not at all, silly.' It's just a word I found in my puzzle,' Alice replied, her pen poised above the paper, ready to strike for another.

In an instant, their tranquil atmosphere fractured like fragile glass, shattered by the shrill ringing of the phone. Alice and Marcus jolted, their eyes meeting in a shared moment of bewilderment. They remained motionless, their gazes locked in a silent exchange, the tension mounting with each passing ring.

Alice's resolve wavered, her features clouding with doubt. 'Should we answer that?' she whispered.

Marcus shook his head, a wry smile on his lips. 'Nah, probably just another telemarketer.' He returned his attention to the small print on his instructions.

Alice, too, retreated to her puzzle, unaware of the impending chain of events and the storm brewing on the horizon.

Mayor Emily Winter's frustration reached its peak, her hand slamming down the receiver on the phone's cradle, the resounding thud echoing through the office. On the other side of the thin wall, Bianca Stollen, Emily's long-suffering receptionist, jolted in her seat, her eyes darting towards Emily's closed door.

Emily's office felt like a pressure cooker, with her frustration simmering just beneath the surface, a slow-burning heat threatening to explode. She didn't want to contact the police and had opted for Jinglebell Sleuths instead. However, nobody seemed to want to pick up the phone on their end. Despite Emily's repeated attempts to reach the detectives, all she encountered was maddening silence, knowing Alice Frost and Marcus Green were likely knee-deep in nothingness. After all, nothing ever happened in Jinglebell – until the past couple of days.

Her lovely Fifi had gone missing. The dog walker, Angela Goldstar, from Jolly Paws Pet Services had arrived at the mansion to collect her. Yet, there was no sign of Fifi. It seemed as if her elderly companion had vanished into thin air, disappearing like magic. Angela had stood at the doorway, scanning the large walled garden for any sign of the missing dog to no avail.

With a scowl, Emily pulled up her emails, singled out the new and strange contact, her fingers dancing over the keypad with lightning speed – *Give it back. I don't care what you do to my reputation. Just, please give it back, and while you're at it, return Fifi too.*

With that, Emily stormed out of her office, the door slamming shut behind her. She cast a despairing look at Bianca, who sat painting her nails an absurd electric banana colour. 'Cancel all my appointments,' Emily snapped. 'I'll be out for the remainder of the day.'

Emily's shiny black heels echoed sharply against the marble floor as she strode through the council building, focused solely on her path. She ignored Nicholas Yuletide's attempts to catch her attention, undeterred by his imposing presence and the cloying aftershave that could fell an elephant from three rooms away.

She reached the towering glass door and bracing herself for the winter chill, stepped gingerly onto the frosty pavement outside, her breath forming clouds in the chilly air. With the elegance of a giraffe on roller skates, she slipped and glided her way to her Mercedes-Benz, cursing the person in charge of de-icing the pavements for not peppering enough salt to prevent slipping.

As she neared the vehicle, something caught her eye – a pristine white envelope jammed between the windscreen and the windscreen wiper. Her curiosity heightened, Emily reached out and plucked the envelope from its perch. With trembling fingers, she tore it open, the crinkle of paper the only sound reaching her ears in the busy carpark. Her heart skipped a beat as she unfolded the contents – a photograph. It depicted her cherished companion, Fifi. A small Bichon Frise with fluffy white fur and soulful eyes. Her joy turned to shock as she noticed something – the photo was paired with a message that sent chills down her spine.

Letters roughly snipped from newspaper headlines spelled out the message, "*If you go to the police, Fifi will be returned paw by paw.*" The threat loomed ominously, casting a cold dread over Emily.

A wave of terror washed over her as she realised her beloved pet was in peril. Blackmail was to be expected for the return of the . . . she couldn't even think it. But not this - not Fifi.

Emily's eyes darted to and fro, searching the bustling street for any sign of the dognapping culprit amidst the merry throng of holiday shoppers. In the distance, she spotted Billy Bobbleton strolling down the road, plastering tickets on the windshields of those who parked on yellow lines.

Without a moment's hesitation, she raced after him, slipping and skidding until she finally caught up with him, breathless. 'Billy,' she called out. 'You have to stop.'

Billy turned around, surprise flitting across his face. 'Mayor Winter, I can't stop. It's my job. This time of the year is when we make the most money for Jinglebell's coffers,' he said, his tone apologetic. 'You see, with the holiday season, folks start parking here deliberately, contributing to the much-needed funds for the turning on of the Jazz-up Jinglebell Christmas lights ceremony. People will be offended if they don't get one of these.' He held up his ticket book. 'The townsfolk proudly display their parking ticket on the mantelpiece beside their Christmas cards,' he added.

'I didn't mean to stop what you were doing,' she said, waving the letter and envelope in the air. 'Did you see anyone hanging around my car? I found this stuck to it.'

After a thoughtful pause, Billy's expression brightened. 'Come to think of it,' he began, 'I did see Arthur Snow stop by it. I thought he was admiring the sleek bodywork. However, he lost interest in it pretty quick when he bumped into Quinten Tinsel.'

A flurry of unsettling thoughts swirled in Emily's mind. Could it be Arthur Snow who left the letter on her car's windscreen? She recalled his lingering resentment after she rejected his romantic advances way back in their teens - a wound that time had failed to heal. Was he also responsible for taking Fifi? Was he the one sending emails while pretending to be Klause? Had Arthur Snow stolen the Snowflake diamond from her safe? Then again, there was a troubled history with Quinten Tinsel as well. Despite his youth, worry lines etched his brow, deepening with each subtle frown whenever Emily attempted to engage with him.

'Are you alright Mayor Winter?' Billy asked.

Emily's mind spun with confusion. 'I could use a drink,' she said, her voice trailing off as she turned away, leaving Billy to ponder her state of mind.

The dim glow of the chandelier cast long shadows in the opulent room, where Arthur Snow reclined on a plush leather chair behind his imposing mahogany desk. He reached for the side drawer, sliding it open. Inside lay one of his prize possessions – a small black book.

Turning to the 'T' section, his finger traced along the rows of neatly written names until he stopped at an entry listed as Trusted Acquaintance. He lifted the receiver from its cradle, his icy blue eyes narrowing in on the number on the page and the numbers he twirled on the phone dial.

'Ah, yes,' he murmured, his voice smooth as silk. 'I need you to dig deeper into Mayor Winter's past. There must be something we can use against her. I want every skeleton in her closet laid bare. How did she manage to pay for her Mercedes-Benz in cash? Something's afoot, and if I'm going to be running against her in the spring elections, I need to be armed with information. Also, I didn't receive the documents you were going to send over with her signature. Please get this to me right away.' A cunning smile spread across his face as he ended the call.

Leaning back in his chair, he contemplated the sinister plan he had devised as a last resort. Not only would he sabotage the Winter Gala, but he would also tarnish Mayor Winter's reputation, casting her as an icy ghoul of the worst kind.

'Yes,' he muttered to himself, 'This will be my masterpiece, and that wearisome woman's name will be lost in a snow globe of time forever.'

Picking up the phone once more, he dialled his contact at the telephone exchange centre. 'Patch me through to a secure line for the following number,' he requested, clearly enunciating each digit.

The dialling tone echoed down the line, until he heard it – a subtle click signalling his connection - away from any prying ears. 'It's me,' Arthur said, his voice dripping with venom. 'Can you create an offshore bank account under the name of Emily Winter? Ensure a significant cash transfer, to be made without leaving an audit trail. I'll fill out any necessary paperwork, including her signature.'

It only took five minutes for the fax machine to beep, producing both a bank account application form and a document with Emily Winter's signature. With the deft stroke of his pen, Arthur printed all the information required in bold black letters before forging Mayor Winter's name on the dotted line.

Arthur's gaze fell to his gleaming Rolex, its polished surface catching the soft lamplight. He cursed silently under his breath. The wristwatch seemed to mock his lack of pace . . . he was running late. The Jinglebell Rocks Charity Supper was about to begin, and every member of the community needed to witness him offering his support to the local orphanage.

Slinging his tweed jacket over his shoulder, he grabbed his chequebook and hurried out. He couldn't shake the image of Mayor Winter's smug smile as she flaunted her wealth. Resolute in his mission to erase it, he envisioned himself swooping in with a larger donation, tripling her paltry offering and wiping her self-satisfied grin off her face once and for all.

As the townsfolk streamed into the Grand Hall for the Jinglebell charity event, they were met with a scene out of a winter wonderland fairy tale. The hall shimmered with hues of colourful fairy lights, their crystals casting prismatic reflections across the polished laminate floor.

Garlands of evergreen boughs filled the air with the crisp scent of pine. At the centre of the room stood a majestic Christmas tree, resplendent with glittering baubles and delicate ornaments. It cast a warm, festive glow that illuminated the faces of those gathered around it.

Tables groaned under the weight of delectable hors d'oeuvres, each piled high with petite vol-au-vents, a few pineapple hedgehogs, and glistening bottles of sparkling Lambrusco. The homemade plum punch added a vibrant splash of colour.

Laughter and chatter blended with the soft melodies of festive music drifting from the hidden Hi-Fi system.

As the lights on the Christmas tree twinkled, the Chief Constable, Holly Sprinkle, held court. Her authoritative presence was softened by a warm smile as she engaged in lively conversation with Alice Frost and Marcus Green, two sleuths whom Arthur held in disdain.

Alice nibbled on a spiced gingerbread cookie, the sweet warmth of cinnamon and nutmeg dancing on her tongue as she savoured the holiday spirit in every bite. 'Back when we were young,' Alice remarked, placing her plate on the table. 'I had Marcus's figure, and he had my hair,' she said, wrestling with her unruly, greying curls to tame them into a ponytail. She chuckled, shooting a teasing glance at Marcus's balding head. 'He looks more like a lamppost than a private detective.'

Alice couldn't help but notice Mayor Winter hovering nearby, her expression betraying a desperate longing to join their light-hearted conversation. As the Mayor hesitated, shifting from foot to foot, Billy Bobbleton stumbled into her, sending his glass of Lambrusco flying. The wine splashed across Emily's red satin dress, leaving a terrible stain and plunging those nearby into an awkward silence.

'I'm so sorry,' Billy exclaimed, his voice rising in panic. 'Let me get some napkins right away.'

'It's alright,' Emily said, with a reassuring smile. 'I have some handkerchiefs in my handbag.' As she reached inside, her fingertips brushed against an envelope – one she hadn't placed there herself. Had someone slipped a second mysterious letter into her bag?

Emily's heart quickened its pace, threatening to break free from her chest. 'Excuse me, she said, flashing a sweet smile to those around her. 'I think I'll nip to the Ladies' room for a moment to rinse this off with some cold water.'

. . .

Arthur Snow lurked in the shadows, his eyes fixed on Emily as she interacted with Billy. A light tingle spread through him at the sight of her discomfort, a cruel smile of satisfaction curling his lips as he observed her every awkward move. His focus shifted as a waiter approached him, extending a small envelope in his white-gloved hand.

'This has just arrived for you, Sir,' he said, with a brisk nod.

Arthur tore open the envelope – *"Emily has lost the prized Snowflake diamond and hasn't reported it to the Council Chambers . . . or the police. Yours, sincerely, Trusted Acquaintance.*

As Nicholas Yuletide, Quinten Tinsel, Billy Bobbleton and Alice Frost happened to glance over at him, Arthur raised his champagne glass in a silent toast – a sly grin plastering his face.

The potpourri in the Ladies' toilets wafted a delightful rose scent, transforming the space into an oasis of floral bliss. Emily sat on one of the plush velvet chaise lounges in the far corner, her fingers twisting her pearl necklace. The latest message depicted Fifi in a different pose, her usual ribbons absent, allowing her fringe to frame her tiny brown eyes.

Once more, the letter was crafted from newspaper clippings arranged below a picture of her beloved pet. The note demanded a five-thousand-pound ransom to be placed in a bag, with the drop-off location to be revealed in the next letter.

As Emily deliberated the implications of the ransom note, her thoughts raced back to the initial letter. Suddenly, a revelation struck her. The letter wasn't a blackmail attempt to ensure her silence about the stolen Snowflake diamond. The kidnapping of Fifi and the theft of the gem were two separate issues.

The tranquillity of the Ladies' room shattered the moment Alice stepped inside, her larger-than-life presence casting a shadow against the opulent backdrop of gilded mirrors. Emily's gaze flicked to Alice's reflection, and her round face stared back.

'Is everything okay?' Alice asked, a sixth sense tingling at the back of her neck.

Emily fell into a heap on the sofa, her sobs racking her slim form, each gasp a holler of despair. She buried her head in her trembling hands, the crumpled envelope nestled between her fingers, drawing Alice's gaze like magnets to metal.

Alice's hand darted forward, snatching the note before Emily could protest. 'What do we have here?' she asked, raising an eyebrow.

The first thing Alice noticed was the missing ribbons usually adorning Fifi's pretty head. Then, the peculiar arrangement of newspaper clippings pieced together to form a ransom demand. 'Is this some kind of early April Fool's joke?' Alice asked.

'I wish it were,' Emily said, pulling herself together. 'This is the second one; the first warned me against involving the police. But . . . I foolishly dismissed it . . . thinking it was tied to another matter. It's unmistakably a kidnapping now.'

'Could you tell me about the other matter? They could be related.'

Emily waved off the suggestion with a flick of her hand. 'Oh, it's nothing really,' she replied, attempting to downplay its importance. Then, with a hint of reluctance, continued. 'I did try calling your office, but no one answered.'

'I'll need the first letter you received,' Alice said, as she tucked the note back into its envelope. Her fingers lingered for a moment on Emily's arm. 'Has anyone else handled this note besides you and me?'

'Only me,' Emily said, with a shiver. 'But I can't shake this feeling off of being watched. What if the sender is aware of our conversation? What might they do to Fifi?' Her voice quivered as she glanced around.

Alice rose from the sofa, and despite short, thick legs, her strides were long. She pushed each toilet door open, one by one, revealing empty cubicles in all five. 'We're in the clear. If anyone happens to be watching when we leave, they'll assume we were two young ladies chit-chatting in the loo.'

Emily's lips twitched, her hand flying to her mouth to stifle the chuckle threatening to escape. 'You always know how to lighten the mood, Alice,' she said, rising from the sofa and making her way to the mirrors. She retrieved a tube of ruby-red lipstick from her handbag and applied it to her pouted lips. 'I must admit, the idea of reliving my youth doesn't hold much appeal,' Emily said, puffing up her heavily lacquered hair, which shimmered high on her head like a fiery comet. 'One more term as Mayor, and then it's retirement for me,' she added, a wistful look in her eyes.

Back in the grand hall, Chief Constable Holly Sprinkle took to the stage. With a light tap to the head of the microphone, she created a loud thud. 'Testing, testing, one two three,' she said, her voice projecting around the room.

Alice's strong grip grabbed Emily's delicate wrist, ushering her to the forefront of the assembled crowd. 'You should be up there with Holly. She's about to thank you for your kind donation,' she said, parting the townsfolk like the bow of a ship cutting through waves.

'Ah, Mayor Winter, there you are,' Holly said, as Emily ascended the stage to join her. The sound of Holly's applause filled the room, quickly joined by the crowd's enthusiastic thunderous clapping. As the townsfolk's appreciation reached a crescendo, Holly raised her hands, gesturing for silence. Gradually, the cheers and whoops subsided, and a hushed anticipation descended.

Emily cleared her throat, took a deep breath and stepped forward to the microphone. 'Thank you,' she began. 'It's been a pleasure serving as Mayor, and I'm honoured to continue to do so, and do all that I can for our wonderful community in Jinglebell. As usual, I will be donating five thousand pounds to the orphanage.

Applause swelled once more as Emily's words resonated with the crowd, their appreciation palpable throughout the Grand Hall. 'And since I'm throwing my hat into the ring for the upcoming elections. I trust I can count on your votes.'

In the midst of the joyous scene, Arthur Snow crept from the shadows, waving his chequebook high above his head. 'Friends of Jinglebell.' His voice boomed without the aid of the microphone. 'I'm happy to donate fifteen thousand pounds to each of our community charities.'

As Arthur spoke, murmurs of surprise rippled through the large hall, all eyes turning to him with curious stares. He continued, pleased to feel the room shift in his direction. 'Let me make it clear,' he said, his tone laced with arrogance,' I will also be putting my name forward for Mayor. It's time things were shaken up around here, and I'm the man to do it.'

Arthur's bold proclamation brought a moment of shock. Whispers of disbelief floated through the air like a soft current, while Emily's face contorted with disgust.

Her eyes narrowed as she exchanged incredulous glances with those nearby. 'And what makes you think you are qualified to lead this town?' she asked, her arms crossed over her chest as she fixed Arthur with a steady stare.

'I wouldn't steal the town's prized snowflake diamond for starters,' he said, his accusatory tone highlighted by a defiant tilt of his chin.

The colour drained from Emily's rouged cheeks. 'I didn't . . . steal it. It was stolen from me,' she whispered, her voice barely heard over the murmurs of the crowd.

Quinten Tinsel stepped forward, hoping to add weight to Arthur's accusations. 'And has this theft been reported to the police?'

'Well, no . . . not yet, 'Emily stuttered, her voice tinged with apprehension.

Quinten shot Arthur a triumphant glance before turning his

attention to Holly, his gaze imbued with a steely resolve that allowed for no opposition. 'Arrest this woman on suspicion of stealing from the townspeople of Jinglebell,' he commanded. 'And look into her finances too, as I'm sure you'll find some disturbing irregularities.' The tone of his voice resembled a command more than a request.

'This is outrageous,' Emily protested, her face a storm of emotions. 'It's plain to see I'm being set up.'

'We should continue this discussion at the station,' Holly said, summoning the policeman on duty with a quick nod.

Emily pointed an accusatory finger at Arthur Snow, her voice rising with indignation. 'You orchestrated this, didn't you?' she said, her eyes narrowing. 'You're framing me because you're gunning for the Mayor's seat. The only way you can win is by tarnishing my reputation.'

The policeman guided Emily through the Great Hall, steering past the crowd of bewildered onlookers. Stepping outside, her legs trembled on the icy path toward the waiting police car. The driver had already fired the engine, its blue light casting an eerie glow on the surrounding snow.

Alice scanned the inquisitive crowd now gathered in the cold outdoors. Her mind worked like a well-oiled machine, cataloguing every detail, every word, and every gesture made.

With a devious grin, Arthur Snow cast a satisfied glance at Quinten Tinsel. Bianca Stollen, her nails painted a striking shade of electric banana, covered her mouth in shock. Angela Goldstar's panicked cries of, 'What happened to Fifi?' echoed through the hall. Beside her, Billy Bobbleton's fingers twitched at his sides, adrift without his customary stack of parking tickets. Nicholas Yuletide kept his distance, dousing himself in cheap cologne, as if trying to wash away any trace of scandal. He, too, met Arthur Snow's gaze, their eyes locking as if bound by a hidden secret.

With determination blazing in her eyes, Alice made a silent vow. She would not rest until she unravelled the truth behind the dark secrets lurking beneath the surface of Jinglebell's idyllic façade.

The next day, there was no time for word searches or shed building instructions. Alice stepped into the office, ready to trade their idle distractions for the weight of her pen and notepad, immersing herself in genuine investigation work.

Shortly after, Marcus arrived, settling at his desk with a strong coffee and the daily newspaper. 'You're in early,' he said.

Alice swooped in, grabbed the paper from his clutches and patted the top of the computer screen on his desk. 'No slacking off for us today. We're going to do some sleuthing.'

'If it's Emily we're looking into,' Marcus said. 'It seems evident she's either lost or stolen the diamond. Why else would she avoid reporting it to the police? I think once Holly has interviewed her, the case will be closed.'

'Remember the other day when the phone rang, and we chose to ignore it?' Alice replied, pacing back and forth. 'That was Emily trying to reach us. If only we'd answered, we would be well ahead on this whole fiasco.'

Marcus leaned forward, his expression thoughtful. 'Go on, tell me more.'

Alice nodded, delighted to have his full attention, and wheeled her chair over to sit beside him. As she spoke, her fingers tapped nervously on the worn surface of Marcus's desk. 'I don't believe Emily stole the diamond. I think she was going to report it missing to us and seek our help,' Alice said, her words falling quicker as she relayed her opinion. 'I think she's concealing something, or perhaps protecting someone.' With a solemn look, Alice plucked her bag from the floor and pulled out a crumpled piece of paper. 'Emily also received a ransom note for Fifi. She handed him the letter.

'Where do we go from here?' Marcus asked, studying the contents of the note.

'Emily said there was a first letter, left on the windscreen of her car. I'll head over to her house and check things out there. Send this one off to your contact at the police department for analysis. Let's see if we can pull off any prints. We need to look at Emily's financial records too.'

As Marcus nodded, Alice added, 'Also, ask around about Arthur Snow's investments while you're at it. How did he manage to build his multi-business empire outside of Jinglebell's parameters?' Her gaze hardened at the mention of Arthur Snow. 'There's something fishy going on with him and Quinten Tinsel - I'm sure of it.'

Alice ventured through the manicured gardens of Emily's mansion, the crunch of her boots on the frost-kissed earth filled the wintry silence. Towering evergreens stretched skyward, their boughs draped in a shimmering cloak of snow. Every breath lingered in the cold air like wisps of white smoke.

Standing on the threshold of the grand arched entryway, Alice felt out of place. She grasped the gleaming brass knocker and struck it against the hardy wood with more force than necessary. Moments later, the door creaked open, revealing a figure shrouded in the dim light of the foyer. Clad in impeccable attire, Noel Crispin, the butler, extended his gloved hand to welcome Alice into Emily's home.

'Thank you for agreeing to meet with me,' Alice said, with a grateful smile as Noel escorted her into the large, luxurious drawing room.

'If it helps in clearing my good lady's name, I'm more than willing to assist,' Noel replied, his concern for Emily's reputation evident.

Alice wandered the length of the large walled library, her fingers trailing along the spines of neatly filed books. The scent of aged paper and leather bindings added to the historical feel of the room. 'You've been with Emily for years,' she began, her voice soft but probing. 'So I understand if this is a challenging time. Did she confide in you about the theft of the Snowflake diamond?'

Noel's expression turned sombre as he shook his head. 'No, she didn't,' he said, his gaze distant - as if reliving the events of that morning. 'But I sensed her distress as she rushed out to the office. It was unlike her to neglect her time in the garden with Fifi, but she dashed out, heedless of the little one's desperate pleas.'

Alice's heart sank at the mention of Fifi's plight. 'And this was the same morning Fifi was dog-napped?'

'Yes,' Noel replied with a nod. 'I was in town when Angela arrived. She has a key and comes and goes quite frequently. But that day, she was in such a state, absolutely terrified of being blamed for Fifi's disappearance and facing Emily's wrath.' He paused, a flicker of hesitation crossing his features. 'Emily has always been kind to me, but she can be hostile to those around her if things don't go her way. Not that it makes her a bad person, just a very ambitious one.'

'Can you show me the safe where the diamond was kept?' Alice asked, then added, 'And I need the first ransom note Emily received.'

'Of course, please follow me,' Noel said, heading towards the door.

Back in the foyer, Alice's attention was drawn to a photo on a nearby table, its silver frame glinting in the lamplight. She picked it up, her eyes tracing the contours of the handsome young man frozen in time. The cotton red hoodie was striking against his olive skin and dark hair. 'Who is this?' she asked, his features triggering a sense of familiarity – the brown eyes, the square jaw – all reminiscent of someone she couldn't quite place.

Alice drove through the gates of Emily's mansion and onto Evergreen Lane, leaving the town behind. In the blink of an eye,

Jinglebell vanished from view, replaced by pristine snowfields and frosted firs glistening like diamonds under the pale winter sun. She stopped at the Cosy Chimney Inn and called her office from the public phone at the bar. 'Hey, Marcus. Can you dig up some information on a chap called Klause Winter? And call the police station - run the name by Holly Sprinkle? See if it triggers any recognition?'

'Will do,' Marcus replied. 'By the way, where're you now?'

'I'm just leaving the Cosy Chimney and heading out to Jolly Paws Pet Services to see if I can catch up with Angela Goldstar,' Alice said. 'I'll keep you posted.'

At Jolly Paws Pet Services, the vibrant blue letters of the sign above the quaint farm building welcomed both canines and their owners with a cheerful invitation. Rows of small stall-like kennels dotted the perimeter, each decked with cosy blankets, food and water bowls. A spacious play area beckoned with an array of colourful obstacles, providing endless fun for furry companions to romp and frolic to their hearts' content.

Alice rattled the door marked Office, and it swung open to reveal a woman standing in the doorway.

'Hello, how can I help you?' she asked, with a friendly smile.

'I'm here to speak with Angela Goldstar,' Alice said, presenting her business card. 'If it's alright, I'd like to have a word with her.'

The woman wiped her sweaty forehead with the sleeve of her woolly jumper. 'Angela's our dog walker, so she doesn't usually work here at the kennels. She services our clients in town. You'll probably find her wandering the streets of Jinglebell searching for Mayor Winter's dog, Fifi. Angela's been distraught since she went missing.'

A sudden bump from the next room drew Alice's attention. 'Is everything alright?'

The woman's gaze snapped to the side, beyond Alice's line of vision. 'One of the pups must have gotten loose. I better go and check,' she said, flexing her fingers.

'Can I have your name, in the event I need to speak with you again?' Alice asked.

'Joy Cracker,' she said, a nervous smile twitching her lips. 'Pop by anytime.'

As Alice walked back to her car, she noticed a dark blue Audi parked discretely behind a hedgerow, away from the main parking area. Peering through its window, she caught sight of a red cotton hoodie draped over the back seat. Pulling out her notepad, she quickly jotted down the registration number of the car before checking the next name on her list.

Nicholas Yuletide settled into his ageing sofa near the crackling coal fire, its warm glow spreading throughout his humble lounge. Christmas trinkets shone from every corner – from twinkling lights to whimsical homemade paper chains. They draped the walls in a riot of colours.

Alice's gaze wandered around the room, pausing on each festive garland. 'You certainly take this time of the year to a new level.'

Nicholas's voice rang with cheer. 'It's the highlight of the year here in Jinglebell. Are you looking forward to the Christmas Gala? Might be a bit of a flop without the snowflake diamond. I still can't believe Emily . . . Mayor Winter would steal such a precious jewel, especially since it belongs to the townsfolk.'

'Nothing has been proven yet as far as I know. I believe the police are still looking into the circumstances of its disappearance.' Alice leaned forward, her eyes narrowing. 'Do you still work closely with Emily at the Council Offices?'

'Well, indeed. We're still quite the duo, steering the bureaucratic maze together. Emily is the strategist, orchestrating our moves with great finesse, while I handle the hands-on tasks. It's a partnership that keeps the wheels turning smoothly, even amidst the festive bustle.'

Alice opened her notebook, her pen hovering above. 'Have you noticed anything or anyone suspicious around the offices lately? Anything that might raise a concern?'

His thin lips formed a straight line as he mulled over Alice's questions. His eyes darted around as if he were wary of being overheard. 'Well,' he started, his voice hesitant. 'There's been a figure lurking across the street opposite the offices. I'd say by the broadness of the shoulders, it's a man. The face is hidden beneath a hoodie, so it's difficult to tell.' He tapped his fingers against the armrest of the sofa. 'I attempted to broach the subject with Mayor Winter yesterday,' Nicholas said with a sigh. 'But she seemed preoccupied, dashing past in a hurry.'

Alice dropped her pen and reached down to pick it up, her eyes caught a splotch of yellow paint marring the otherwise pristine sheepskin rug. Nicholas followed her gaze, a lopsided grin spreading across his face. 'I made a mess. It's a lesson learned - never paint paper chains unless sitting at a table.'

'One last question,' Alice asked, secretly sniffing the air. 'What kind of aftershave are you wearing?'

Alice stepped into the bustling Bells and Beans café, instantly swathed by the tantalising aroma of freshly brewed coffee and the scent of savoury toasted scones. A flutter of excitement rose in her stomach as she perused her options, settling on a steaming cappuccino, a crisp salad roll, and a large bar of creamy chocolate. With refreshments in hand, she returned to her car, the gentle hum of the engine providing a comforting warmth against the chilly winter scenery outside.

Angela Goldstar shattered her blissful lunch break by darting around the corner, her voice escalating to a fever pitch as she called for Fifi at the top of her lungs. Then a tap on her side window startled her. Alice jumped, nearly spilling the hot drink over her lap. But her tension melted away when she spotted Bianca Stollen standing there, hugging a to-go coffee cup in her hands. As Alice rolled down the window, she couldn't help but shiver as the cold air stole away the cocoon of heat she had created.

'Sorry if I gave you a fright,' Bianca said, taking a sip of the warm liquid. 'There's been a rumour circulating we're being watched. Some creepy person has been spotted staring at the city chambers from across the road, wearing a red hoodie. It seemed to freak Emily out, especially when I told her the hoodie's colour. Do you think I should go to the police with this information?'

'Yes, anything you tell them might be relevant to what has happened,' Alice said, then asked, 'How well do you know Nicholas Yuletide?' Her mind flashed back to the yellow stain on his carpet on seeing the glitzy yellow paint of Bianca's fingernails.

Bianca's cheeks flushed crimson. 'We've been dating for six months now and would love to get married. But, weddings are so expensive. The Sleigh Bell Hotel provided a quote for an evening reception, but there's no way on our wages we could afford it. Nicholas keeps asking Emily for a pay rise, but she completely ignores him. It's cheeky of her, considering he does most of the work while she takes all the credit.'

Alice's first thought was that there might still be hope for her, watching Bianca and Nicholas embark on a relationship in their late forties. If anything were ever to happen between her and Marcus, she would need to start dropping some serious hints.

'Can I ask you something?' Bianca said, continuing without waiting for an answer. 'What will happen if Angela manages to find Fifi - will the police drop that part of the investigation?'

'You would need to direct that question to the Chief Constable. I'm heading over to the police station now, so I could ask . . . if you like?'

. . .

The police station was packed with commotion. Holly had allocated additional manpower to aid in the search for the missing diamond. The influx of new bodies introduced a heavy smell of freshly brewed coffee, mingling with the lingering scent of cigarette smoke.

Alice's gaze was drawn to Billy Bobbleton, who sat across from a police sketch artist in a small corner of the large room. The artist's pencil moved furiously across the page as a wide-eyed Billy leaned forward checking the progress.

'What's happening here?' Alice asked, grabbing a nearby chair and dragging it across to join the two men.

Billy sounded pleased with himself. 'I noticed this suspicious-looking person watching Emily get into her car two days ago. He appeared to be mesmerised, walking out onto the middle of the road until her car disappeared from his sight. Then, I spotted him again this morning, hanging around outside the police station.'

Alice nodded, keen to know more. 'And was it this morning that you managed to get a good look at him – enough to provide the police with a sketch of his face?' she asked.

'Well,' Billy continued, a touch of frustration in his voice, 'I did approach him, but he wasn't too friendly. As soon as I got close, he bolted off down the street. But, I saw enough to be able to help.'

Alice examined the police sketch Billy had helped provide. The figure drawn bore a striking resemblance to Klause Winter, the man in the photograph on Emily's table. However, in this version, he appeared older, with lines etched around his eyes and wrinkles creasing his forehead.

A door to the side creaked open. 'Alice,' Holly called, her tone inviting. 'Care to join me in interview room one?'

'Can I take this?' Alice asked, lifting the sketch from the artist. 'I'll bring it straight back.'

. . .

Emily's eyes glistened with tears. She sat hunched over the table clutching tissues in her trembling hands. The interview room itself seemed to hold its breath, suspended in a time warp of sadness.

'Alice, I'm glad you could join us,' Holly said, leaning back in her chair. 'Emily mentioned she granted permission for your assistance, and we're all eager to uncover the truth behind what has happened.'

Alice placed the artist's impression of Klause Winter on the table. 'Can you take a good look, Emily?'

Emily gasped, her eyes widening, as her face turned pale. With a choked sob, she buried her face in her hands. 'It's him,' she said, her voice quivering. 'He's back.'

Just as Alice was about to ask further questions about Klause, the phone on the desk erupted with a sharp ring. Holly quickly picked it up and learned that Marcus Green was on the line from the Sleuths office. 'It's for you,' she said, handing the handset to Alice.

Marcus's voice was pitched higher than usual. 'You won't believe this,' he said, the words spilling down the line. 'Word is going around - Angela Goldstar has found Fifi. She's heading to the police station right now.' Alice was about to hang up when Marcus added. 'I've also faxed over some financial records to the police station for you to look at.'

Alice turned to Holly. 'Sorry, but I need to step out for a moment. However, as soon as I come back, I want to know all about Klause Winter.'

Fifi bounded into the precinct, her tail wagging with infectious joy. Alice couldn't help but smile at her antics, as Fifi showered everyone in reach with affectionate licks and joyful barks. Despite the gravity of the situation surrounding her owner, Fifi seemed blissfully unaware, her bright eyes filled with nothing but pure happiness.

Alice scooped the wriggling dog into her arms, loving the tiny wet kisses she received. 'So, she just turned up in the garden?' she asked Angela, her attention returning to the matter at hand.

'Yes,' Angela nodded, her expression serious. 'I thought I should bring her down to the station right away.'

A chemical smell wafted from Fifi's paws catching Alice's attention. She dipped her head for a closer sniff, her mind racing with possibilities. 'It's like she's been strolling through some sort of substance.' On closer examination, Alice spotted a minuscule speck of yellow paint, overlooked on one of the claws on her back left paw.

'Here, take her,' Alice said, passing Fifi to one of the policemen. 'I don't need to tell you to have all four paws photographed and processed for forensic evidence. Her mind was already racing on to the next steps. 'Also, have someone lift some of the chemical residue from her claws to determine what it is,' she added, believing they were finally making headway in unravelling the truth behind Fifi's abduction.

The curious policeman cocked his head slightly to the side and asked. 'Care to share what's brewing inside that brilliant mind of yours, Alice?'

A warm smile spread across her face. 'If my hunch is on target, you'll discover it's nail polish remover,' she replied, her confidence growing. 'Now, I believe my colleague sent over some information for my attention. Can you point me in the direction of your fax machine?'

As Alice re-entered the interview room, the soft hum of fluorescent lights was the only sound to be heard. Emily had regained her composure, and Holly sat reading Emily's statement.

'Welcome back,' Holly said, patting the seat beside her for Alice to take her place. 'Emily has given a written account.' She tapped the paper in front of her. 'But before she signs it, we want to clarify a few issues.'

Alice reached into her pocket and pulled out her notepad. 'Could we start by talking about Klause Winter?' she asked. 'I noticed a photograph of a young man in your house. Billy Bobbleton mentioned encountering the same man on the street.' She pushed the sketch in front of Emily. 'Or rather, his older self.'

Clutching her chest, Emily closed her eyes and took a deep breath. 'Klause was my husband. At first, all was well – until he began to stifle my ambitions. We were off the coast of Corfu, on our yacht, A Splice of Heaven, when he got drunk and fell overboard, never to be seen again.'

'I doubt he's come back from a watery grave to haunt you?' Alice said, wondering where the man had hidden himself all these years.

'Emily's face contorted in horror. 'It started with emails,' she said, her voice quivering. At first, I thought it was a prank - someone pretending to be him and trying to blackmail me. The emails said if I didn't confess to what I'd done, I would be sorry.' She paused, gripping the edge of the table for support. 'But if someone has seen him, then he must be alive. It has to be him who took the Snowflake diamond. It's his vengeance for me living life to the fullest without him.'

'Why would he appear now and what is it you were supposed to have done? It doesn't make any sense,' Alice said, her frustration bubbling. 'I'll need access to your email account.'

'I didn't do anything. The crew we had on the yacht with us witnessed his falling. Holly knew him,' Emily continued, her eyes meeting the Chief Constables. 'And can testify to the monster he turned into. He lived a double life, with a family I knew nothing of until his demise. Anyway, seven years after his disappearance, he was legally declared dead. His estate was settled, and I became a very wealthy woman, also fighting off a legal claim from his other family who felt they should have inherited everything from his death. I returned to Jinglebell to start afresh, and Holly helped me in my political pursuits. If Klause hadn't met his end on that boat, I'd still be trapped in the same old cycle.'

'So how do we go about retrieving the Snowflake diamond?' Holly asked. 'Considering our prime suspect is still supposedly resting at the bottom of the ocean.'

'There's another matter we must address too,' Alice said, sliding a copy of an offshore bank account statement across the table. 'How do you account for this, and the substantial sum of money it contains?'

As the document exchanged hands, tension filled the room, each glance and gesture fraught with suspicion. 'It looks like my signature on these papers,' Emily said, a look of disbelief clouding her face. 'But I promise, this is not mine, and I have no clue why this account is set up in my name.'

'I have an idea,' Alice said, facing Holly with a formidable gleam in her eye.

'Tomorrow, you should hold a press conference with all the local journalists. Declare you've successfully recovered the Snowflake diamond and that the perpetrators behind Fifi's kidnapping are now in custody. Tell the people of Jinglebell that all will be revealed at the Christmas Gala.'

'And what do we hope to achieve by doing that?' Holly asked.

'Leave it with me, I'm still working on it,' Alice replied.'

The Grand Hall shimmered with festivity as the townsfolk gathered for the Christmas gala, the most festive evening in the whole of Jinglebell. Alice couldn't help but think more people were attending than usual, all desperate to hear the outcome of the past events.

Following Alice's detailed instructions to Holly, police officers took up strategic positions around the building, effectively sealing off any possible escape routes for her targets. With the attendees mingling unaware, Alice seized the moment and stepped nervously up to the microphone.

'Ladies and gentlemen of Jinglebell,' she began, her voice carrying an anxious tremor. At the door, Marcus flashed a thumbs-up, hoping his encouragement would help. 'I'm pleased to announce Fifi has been safely returned. However, I must confess, we've told a little white lie to gather everyone here tonight. The kidnappers have yet to be apprehended.'

As Alice's revelations sank in, murmurs swelled around the hall with surprise and speculation. Some exchanged incredulous glances while others moved closer to the stage.

With a dramatic pause, Alice revealed, 'The culprit who took Fifi was none other than Bianca Stollen.' As she spoke, her gaze fixed on Bianca, who shifted uncomfortably under the scrutiny. 'I suspect, in moments of boredom, while you had her captive, you painted Fifi's claws with your electric banana nail varnish. However, your attempts to remove all the colouring when you wanted to return her failed, as you missed a tiny spec on her back left paw.'

A flush of indignation heated Bianca's cheeks. Her eyes flashed with fury as she protested. 'This is preposterous.'

Alice continued. 'I believe the paws were painted inside the home of your accomplice – Nicholas Yuletide. You sloppily dropped nail varnish on his sheepskin rug.' She paused, her gaze locking with Nicholas. 'Nicholas claimed he was painting paper chains, but these were made of coloured cardboard and didn't need painting.'

The Great Hall fell into a hush as Bianca and Nicholas grappled to find the right response.

Nicholas's jaw clenched, his eyes narrowing as the accusation landed. He shifted uneasily, grasping for words that wouldn't come. Beside him, Bianca drew a sharp breath, their shared guilt thick and unspoken between them.

'And let's not forget the smell of aftershave.' Alice

continued in a steady tone. 'The scent lingered in the safe where Emily kept the ransom letter she received.' Alice allowed the significance of her words to sink in before delivering the final blow. 'The same scent - Mistletoe Magic - that Nicholas is wearing tonight. I believe he was the one who crafted the ransom notes, leaving that distinctive fragrance on the paper.'

As gasps and murmurs followed, Nicholas finally found his voice. 'Why on earth would Bianca and I want to kidnap Fifi?'

'That's simple. You needed the money to fund your dream wedding reception. I checked with the Sleigh Bell Hotel, and the cost given was exactly the same sum as the ransom demand for Fifi. Emily repeatedly refused to approve the pay raise you needed. So, between you, you concocted a plan of dognapping to finance your special day.'

Bianca's voice sounded more like a whine. 'How could you think that? We would never sink so low as to harm Fifi.'

'I never claimed you intended to cause Fifi harm. I believe you felt sorry for Emily after finding out about the missing Snowflake diamond and had second thoughts. That's why you released Fifi back into the care of Angela in Emily's absence.'

Amidst the rising tension, Angela Goldstar's voice sliced through the room like a blade.

'That's all well and good, and I'm so happy Fifi is safe. But, what about the Snowflake diamond?'

'This puzzle was a little more difficult, but it's as plain as the nose on my face.' Alice said. 'On checking several documents and email messages, it was noted that paperwork with Emily's signature was sent over to Arthur Snow by none other than Nicholas Yuletide, signed off as Trusted Acquaintance.' Her gaze lingered on Nicholas. 'You were so sure of your capabilities and didn't think an audit trail would expose your deceit of sending confidential documents outside of chamber business. I can only presume financial gain was given for your services - perhaps to pay for your honeymoon.'

Several voices now rang out. 'But what's that got to do with the missing diamond?'

Alice refused to be rushed and pressed on at her own pace. 'Arthur Snow, in an act of fraud, forged Emily's signature onto an offshore bank account, which Quinten Tinsel, with his shady reputation, helped to organise. The Financial Crimes Unit are tracing back the document and its timeline, and the signature on it has been sent away for forensic testing.'

Arthur's face turned a deep red, looking ready to burst, with beads of sweat gathering on his brow. He lashed out his denial. 'This is utter nonsense and I'll be seeking legal advice for slander.' His clenched fists hung by his side. 'How dare you make such accusations, Alice Frost.' Beneath his bluster lay a hint of desperation, the realisation of impending consequences dawning upon him.

'Did Arthur steal the diamond?' Angela called out, her impatience growing.

'No, Arthur is guilty of one thing only - ambition. He wanted to become Mayor at any cost. Alice paused, her eyes meeting Arthur's. 'Not only that, he never got over Emily's rejection of his romantic advances, her choosing to marry Klause Winter over him. He's held an unhealthy grudge since. Alice gripped the microphone stand. 'His desire to see Emily's downfall no matter what, was his driving force, and was desperate to step in and manage the political fallout.'

Angela crossed her arms and tapped her foot. 'So, who stole the Snowflake diamond?' she shouted.

Alice scanned the room, looking for the thief. 'Quinten Tinsel is the culprit. He stole the Snowflake diamond,' she called out, meeting his steely stare.

Quinten's mask of calm shattered, his features contorted in anger as the accusation pierced through his defences. 'You have no proof of any wrongdoing on my part. The accusation I stole the diamond is baseless and absurd.' His voice wavered, revealing the crack in his bravado as he did his best to maintain his composure. 'What motive would I have to steal the town's gem?'

'Quinten, you are the love child of Klause Winter and Joy Cracker. After Klause died, your mother lacked financial support, leading to your adoption by the Tinsels. Years later, you discovered your birth mother, who informed you of your true heritage.'

The room descended into a stunned silence, jaws dropping as the revelation sounded through the space. It felt like a bombshell had detonated in their midst, leaving doubt and astonishment scattered in its wake.

'I tracked down your birth certificate,' Alice continued. 'There's also a slight resemblance between you and Klause. I noticed this from a photograph Emily kept, where Klause was wearing a red hoodie. I believe you were trying to impersonate the late Klause Winter to frighten Emily into repaying insurance money you believe was stolen from you and your mother. Additionally, you saw the gem as your rightful inheritance, as it was your great-grandfather who bequeathed the gem to the people of Jinglebell.'

'I've never heard such a load of rubbish,' Quinten yelled.

'I noticed a car parked at the Jolly Paws Pet Services, registered to you. Laid out on the back seat was a red hoodie, which you have been wearing about town. I believe you bribed Billy Bobbleton into corroborating a fabricated sighting of Klause Winter, and had him describe to the police artist a version of an older Klause. I'm sure if we do a thorough search of Jolly Paws Pet Services, the diamond will turn up.' Her gaze found Billy Bobbleton's. 'I asked around town, and no one else claimed to have seen a man in a red hoodie loitering outside the police station on the day Billy claims he was.'

'Is there anything else?' Angela called out, her expression showing a hint of satisfaction.

'Back to Fifi. Once we retrieve fingerprints from the second note slipped into Emily's handbag, I'm certain we'll find Billy

Bobbleton's prints on the envelope. It all felt too staged - the way he toppled over, spilling his drink on Emily while fumbling around. Billy must have been bribed to take part, but he's the only one who can answer that question.'

Billy's head drooped like a wilting flower, his face full of remorse. Alice knew it wouldn't be too difficult for Holly to pull a confession from him on the part he played.

'I think we've heard enough,' Holly said, joining Alice's side and giving her a hearty pat on the back. 'Arrest all the suspects and take them to the station,' she called, signalling to the officers at the back of the hall. 'I'm confident we'll find the Snowflake diamond once the search warrants come through.'

Life in Jinglebell returned to its familiar rhythm. Emily's reunion with Fifi brought joy to the town, and her re-election as Mayor was met with the town's delight. The Snowflake diamond found a new home, safely nestled in the vault of Jinglebell's bank. Alice and Marcus were honoured with several awards for their exemplary investigative work, establishing Jinglebell Sleuths as a serious crime-stopping entity.

As for Alice Frost, her journey took an unexpected turn. Walking down the aisle, she felt ready to embrace a new chapter in her life - as Mrs Alice Green. The echoes of the past mystery faded, replaced by the promising whispers of their future. With each step, she left behind a world of intrigue, stepping into a life filled with warmth, love and endless possibilities. This new beginning marked not just a change in her name, but a transformation in her heart and soul.

And with joyous Jinglebell cheer, the town thrived, its spirit bright and enduring.

BIO:

Having had a passion for reading and writing since an early age, this passion has only grown over the years. Marti M. McNair has been writing since she could pick up a pen and after her children flew the nest she turned to writing seriously. Her main focus is writing for a YA audience, and her books feature dystopian settings, dark political undercurrents and places her characters in precarious situations which tests them to the limit. She was the winner of the prestigious Scottish Association of Writers, Barbara Hammond Prize. She is also a partner in Auscot Publishing and retreats and a graphic designer for Writers' narrative eMagazine.

https://www.martimcnair.com

Chapter Five

RECIPES

Wendy H. Jones and Sheena Macleod

Corned Beef Stovies (serves 4-6)

Corned beef stovies is a simple Scottish dish often served at ceilidhs, functions and as a warming meal at any time of the day or year. Stovies are easy to make. This is a recipe for corned beef stovies, but most other types of beef can be substituted instead.

Ingredients

1 large onion (chopped)

Lard or beef dripping

650 grams of large potatoes (Preferably Maris Piper) peeled and cut into round slices (not too thin)

Salt and pepper to taste

Beef stock (water and beef stock cube will do)

340 grams of corned beef (1 can or fresh slices)

Method

Melt the dripping or lard in a large saucepan. Add the

chopped onions and fry for a couple of minutes. Add the sliced potatoes and blend in with the onions, keeping the pot on the heat. Blend in a third of the corned beef. Season to taste. Add the beef stock (to cover just over three-quarters of the way up the onion, potato and corned beef mix). Cover with the saucepan lid. Bring to the boil and turn the heat down. Simmer until the potatoes have broken down and the liquid has been absorbed (around 30-40 minutes). Five minutes before the stovies are ready, blend in the remainder of the corned beef.

Season to taste with salt and pepper. Serve with oatcakes.

Steak Pie

Steak pie is a traditional dish, most often served at Hogmanay or New Year's Day in Scotland. It is also a popular dish to serve during the festive season or at any time of the year.

Serves 6

Ingredients

425g puff pastry rolled to fit over the pie dish

800g lean stewing steak – cubed

1 large onion - chopped

1 teaspoon wholegrain mustard

30g Cornflour or plain flour (seasoned with salt and pepper to taste)

Dash of Worcestershire sauce

1 Oxo cube (or other beef stock cube)

2 tablespoons of olive or vegetable oil

600ml boiling water

Method

Dip the cubes of stewing steak in the seasoned flour to give a light coating

Brown the coated stewing steak in the olive oil on a medium heat (folding to prevent sticking)

Add the chopped onion and continue to brown for about 5 minutes

Add the Worcestershire sauce

Add the wholegrain mustard and continue to stir

Add the crumbled stock cube

Add enough water to just cover the meat (around 600ml) and stir

Bring to the boil and cook for at least 2 hours on a low heat

Cover and leave to cool. Place in the fridge overnight (this ensures the meat is tender)

Bring the meat out of the fridge, bring to the boil and simmer for 45 minutes.

Place the meat mix in a pie dish and leave to cool for at least 30
minutes.
Preheat the oven to 220 °C (200 °C fan assisted or gas mark 6)
Cover the pie dish with the rolled out puff pastry. Trim around
the edges. (I use a ceramic magpie in the centre of the dish to
hold the pastry up. If not using this, create a small hole in the
centre of the pastry to allow the steam to escape.)
Cook in the centre of the oven for 30 minutes, or until the
pastry is golden brown.
Serve the steak pie with potatoes (mashed, boiled or roasted)
and vegetables (usually carrots and any green vegetables that are
in season).

Festive Sausage Meat and Orange Stuffing (for chicken or turkey)

1 finely chopped onion (small)
350 g sausage meat
Seasoning to taste
2 finely chopped garlic cloves
Juice squeezed from 1 orange
1 beaten egg
Half a cup of rolled Oats
Add mixed herbs to taste

Method
Place the sausage meat in a bowl and break up with your hands
Add the chopped onion, beaten egg, herbs, seasoning and mix
with your hands
Add the rolled oats and orange juice and continue to mix. (If the
mixture is too moist, add more rolled oats).
Stuff the chicken or turkey with the mixture and cook as
instructed.

Quick Lentil, Turkey and Ham Soup

Once Christmas is over most of those who did all the cooking are looking for ways to ease the pressure for a few days and use up all those leftovers. This really is a quick and easy recipe. No preparation, peeling or cutting. As a bonus it is completely gluten free. It is filling, tasty, cheap to make (after the excesses of Christmas) and, above all, quick.

Ingredients
1 large tin of peeled potatoes
2 small tins of carrots
1 cup lentils (that's a British teacup not the US measurement)
2 stock pots or stock cubes - vegetable or ham
Water to fill a large saucepan
Leftover gammon and turkey
Salt and pepper

Method
Open the tins of potatoes and carrots
Place them in a bowl and blend using a hand blender
Add them to a large saucepan with the lentils
Melt down the stock pots or cubes into a pint of boiling water
Add the stock to the saucepan
Add the ham and turkey
Add salt and pepper to taste
Add boiling water to fill the saucepan and stir
Bring to the boil
Simmer with a lid on for about 1 hour

Serve warm with crusty bread or gluten free bread

Best paired with reading a book.

COZY CRAFTY CRIMES

Coming soon from Scott and Lawson Publishing

Welcome to the world of *Cozy Crafty Crimes* where stitches move, glue sticks snap, and murder is always handmade. Set in the world of crafting, each story weaves a tale of mystery, mischief, and creativity. Whether it's cross stitch hiding more than just stitches, or beaded jewellery holding a deadly clue, these amateur sleuths use more than just their crafting skills to untangle the truth. Perfect for fans of cozy mysteries, clever puzzles, and a healthy dollop of crafting charm, this anthology proves that in the crafting world, danger is always just a stitch away.

ACKNOWLEDGMENTS

Thank you to my readers who embrace any book I bring out. You are all amazing.

Thank you also to my coauthors in this book - Marti M. McNair and Sheena Macleod for embracing any book suggestion I throw at them. No matter the topic they rise to the challenge. All writers should have such writing friends in their corner.

Thanks must also go to the members of City Writers, History Writers, Angus Writers' Circle and Ayr Writers for cheering us on and consistently helping others to develop as writers. Writing groups are the backbone of writers everywhere and I salute them.

OTHER COZY MYSTERY BOOKS BY SCOTT AND LAWSON PUBLISHING

Antiques and Alibis

A Right Cozy Christmas Crime

A Right Cozy Culinary Crime

Coming soon

Cozy Crafty Crimes

A Right Cozy Historical Crime

A Right Cozy Library Crime

www.ingramcontent.com/pod-product-compliance
Lightning Source LLC
Chambersburg PA
CBHW032017180726
48283CB00008B/2720